Along Came a

BOOKS BY LINDA WELCH

Along Came a Demon

Whisperings book one

Linda Welch

Whisperings: Along Came a Demon
Linda Welch

Cover by Flip City Books / http://flipcitybooks.com
Tiff photo by Jeffrey Banke / dreamstime.com

November 2009
Printed in the United State of America

ISBN 1449590845
EAN-13978144590840

When people talk of ghosts I don't mention
the apparition by which I am haunted, the
phantom that shadows me about the
streets. . . .

Logan Pearsall Smith

Chapter One

—♈—

"There's a naked woman in the garden," Jack said.

"Ung?" I mumbled, which was about as coherent as I got at seven in the morning. I glanced through the diamond-paned kitchen window. Yep. Naked woman standing on the grass. I didn't recognize her. I groped my way to the counter and hit the button on the coffeemaker, glad I remembered to load it up the night before. The programmable timer hadn't worked for months, and the less time I spent in that no-man's land between getting out of bed and sucking down my first cup, the better.

"Don't you think that's a bit odd?" Jack insisted.

Happily, I was not slugging back my first caffeine fix of the day, or I would have snorted coffee. Odd? When was anything in my life *not* odd? I lolled over the counter as the first drop of water hit the grounds and the truly wonderful aroma of coffee laced with caramel permeated the air.

"A naked *wet* woman in the garden. Dripping wet," he emphasized.

I sighed and turned to lean my spine on the counter. I would rather she were an escaped lunatic who wandered into the neighborhood than what she really was. Although how she could be wet on a chilly November morning was anyone's guess.

"I've been watching her from the bedroom window," Mel said, coming through the door from the hallway, mussing up her permanently mussed red hair with one hand. "She's been standing there, wet, for half an hour."

Not a disoriented stranger in the wrong backyard. Not an escaped loony. Worse. One of them. I sighed again. I did not want to deal with her this early in the morning. "She'll have to wait till *after* I have my coffee."

I didn't want to deal with her, period. I'd just signed off on an unpleasant case and looked forward to a break. Warren Bigger of Ogden reported his wife missing. She went to visit a girlfriend and never came back. He called the friend, but she said she didn't see Monica and did not arrange to meet her. Twenty-four hours later, Warren and the boys were frantic and he called the police. Search parties were organized and leads investigated. Warren stood outside his house, looking solemn, his sons at his side as he spoke to reporters. One of the boys couldn't take it and shook with tears. Sympathy poured in from the community. And I had to go stomp on everyone's good intentions and commiseration by finding Monica's body and fingering Warren as her killer.

I almost gave up after I questioned every dead person in Ogden—and there are a lot of them—and got nowhere. But I methodically went from one to another leading away from the city. Then I talked to Sheila. She saw Warren and Monica take the onramp and head toward Brigham on Interstate 15, the same morning Monica was supposed to be with her girlfriend and the boys were in school. Philip saw them turn off Highway 13 west of Corinne. Finding Monica in the desert took me less than an hour; she was the only woman standing on flat terrain with her hands and ankles tied and a flour sack on her head, right over where her body lay. She told me who killed her. DNA evidence did the rest.

So now the Bigger twins were in foster care, the last place I wanted any kid to be, but would soon be given into the custody of their maternal grandparents, which eased Monica's anguish. Their dad was in the state penitentiary. Hopefully, he would end his days there and Monica could go on to where the shades of the dead go.

I wanted to sit out the morning in the silence of my kitchen, drink strong coffee, maybe clean out my old pink refrigerator, and make a pan of Louisiana bread pudding with whiskey sauce.

No such luck.

Jack sniffed condescendingly, went back to the kitchen table and stooped over the newspaper I picked up on the way home last night, his long brown hair flopping over his brow into his eyes. Mel stood at his shoulder.

Jack's hair permanently flops in startled pale-blue eyes. Mel's hair is always mussed up, as if she just got out of bed, or battled a strong wind. She rakes at it, or tries to smooth it down, but it never changes. Mel's freckled face wears the same apprehensive expression as Jack's does.

I opened the newspaper, then turned back to the counter to fill my mug with precious liquid. I got liquid creamer from the refrigerator, added a good dollop to the coffee, and took my mug to the window. I watched the woman as I sipped. This *was* kind of strange, or I should say stranger than normal. They always remained at their place of departure and this one sure did not depart from my backyard, unless I missed some bizarre event during the night. And why dripping wet? It indicated drowning, but she couldn't have drowned out there.

She looked right at me.

"Ahem!" from Jack.

I stepped to the table, flipped to the next page for him and took a seat, then nursed my mug in both hands. "So what's new with the world?"

"Unfortunately, our provincial little paper doesn't often mention the world," Jack said with a sneer in his voice. "However, you might be interested to know there was a death in the apartments."

"The apartments? You mean. . . ?" I jogged my head.

"Yes. Those apartments. The ones behind us."

"Coralinda Marchant," Mel added helpfully as she peered near-sightedly at the newspaper. "Found dead in her bathtub."

I twisted to look through the window at the tall, dark-haired, wet woman in my backyard. I took another sip of coffee. "What a coincidence."

Now I really did not want to go outside. "Do they know who killed her?"

"No mention of murder. The police are in their no-comment mode," Jack informed me.

"Then they're stalling. She was murdered."

"Cops? Useless!" Jack opined too vehemently. I internally winced, recognizing a lead-in to one of his totally unfunny jokes. They always involve dead people in some way.

"Did you hear the one about the Irish cop? A newcomer said he'd heard about a lot of criminal activity in the area, but it seemed like a quiet little place to him. So the cop tells him, 'Ah, to be sure, we haven't buried a living soul in years.'"

This had to be his fifth rendition of the same, stale old joke.

Mel wrapped her arms over her stomach and deadpanned, "Oh, Lord! she says, clutching her stomach and rolling on the ground with unrestrained mirth."

"You've heard it before," Jack stated.

"Why would you think that?"

Tsking, I put my mug on the table and pulled the paper to my side. Coralinda Marchant: single, thirty-two, lived alone, worked as a secretary at a storage facility on West Canal. A neighbor found her when he saw her apartment door wide open and couldn't resist a snoop; two days ago, on November 17th. They estimated her death as the evening of November 16th.

I pushed the paper back to Jack, turned to the next page for him and tucked my feet up on the rungs of the chair, wishing I put slippers on over my socks. The sun would soon rise above the peaks and flood the kitchen with light and warmth, but until then the inadequate heating left it cool, and the floor felt icy. The radiant heating in my house is old. It is also noisy, popping and crackling at odd hours of the day and night. One day, when I strike it rich—ha ha—I will replace the heating system. Until then, a cold day in mid-November tends to worm its way inside.

A redbrick cottage built in the post-World War II era, my house is small and well built, boasting the original wooden floors and window frames. My favorite rooms, the kitchen and bathroom, are large, and in winter the warmest rooms in the house, the bathroom big enough for my treadmill and TV to fit in with room to spare. I can jog for hours and watch my favorite shows at the same time.

I have to keep in shape. At six-foot-four and slim, my muscle will go to fat if I don't take care of my body, then I'll look like a great lump. I used to be fanatical about exercise, but when my special little talent reared its ugly head, for a while there I lost interest in just about everything except hiding away from the outside world. Seeing the sorry—okay, flabby—shape I was in, helped pull me out of it.

I drained my mug, leaned over it so I could see through window. She was still here, but now she wandered in tight little circles.

It did not make sense. Why—more importantly, how—did dead Coralinda Marchant end up in my yard?

On a half-acre of land at the end of a cul-de-sac, the house butts right up to the curb, with a narrow strip of grass either side and in front where Beeches Street begins a winding descent to Clarion. The woman stood in the middle of the strip on the north side of the house, hands hanging loose at her sides, waiting.

I walked beside the house, my shoes leaving tracks in a thin coat of frost. Hesitating at the corner, I braced for a vision. I don't always see a shade's death, but when I do it literally flashes on the insides of my eyelids like a flickering movie. Even though I know I watch the last moments of a person's life, I think I could learn to live with it as there is a kind of detachment, if not for the accompanying emotion. I feel what they feel and I will never become accustomed to that.

I see what they see. Except for when they are taken from behind, I see the face of their killer.

But nothing came. That's always a relief, but can make discovering what happened to a shade harder, because they are not always sure themselves.

One of the first things I learned about talking with the dead is you do not offer them information. You do not put words in their mouths. If they are confused and you say, "Can you get a message to my Aunt Bertha?" they are just as likely to say they can, because they want to please you. They figure if they please you, you will talk to them again.

So I walked up to the woman I presumed to be Coralinda Marchant and stopped in front of her with one eyebrow hiked like a question mark. The early morning chill bit at my exposed face and hands. I wrapped my arms around myself to stifle a shiver.

I wasn't sure, but I thought tears mingled with the water on her face.

"Thank you," she whispered.

I once asked a spirit why he whispered to me, why they all did. He said he didn't whisper, he spoke in a perfectly normal voice. To me, they seem to whisper.

Her voice was rather high, the sort which could become piercing if she were excited and talking a mile a minute. Dark-brown hair clung to a pointed face and almost down to the waist of a tall, slim, lanky body with small breasts and narrow hips. Thick brown lashes framed huge blue eyes. Not beautiful, but attractive enough to turn a man's head as she walked past him. Just my opinion. The water on her fascinated me; her entire body, every strand of her hair, each individual eyelash. I expected it to drip off, but it coated her like a sheath.

"I'm Lindy Marchant. I live . . . lived on the third floor," she went on, flicking one hand back over her shoulder to indicate the apartment complex behind her.

At least she knew she was dead. Sometimes they don't.

"I've seen you walking the neighborhood and thought I recognized you. I saw your picture in a newspaper when I lived in New Jersey, when you helped the police with the Telford murder. It said you're a psychic detective. I thought, how neat, a psychic, and she lives near me."

Ah, the Telford case, my little piece of notoriety. It involved a meat packer named—wait for it—Mark Butcher, a 1965 Mustang Shelby Fastback, a panicked seventeen-year-old and a clever, panicked father who did not want his boy in the hands of evil law enforcement; a smart county sheriff who stewed over the case for six months before making a call to his old friend Mike Warren, and little old me.

When I work with other PDs, like Clarion they try to keep me under the radar, but a resident of tiny Telford, New Jersey, thought she knew what I did for the police. She told her brother, the editor-cum-reporter-cum-everything else of the Telford Times. He got a picture of me and wrote a story. I'm glad the national newspapers didn't pick it up.

So Lindy lived in New Jersey and just happened to read the article. People like to debate fate and coincidence. I don't believe in fate, and coincidence can be a huge pain in the butt as far as I'm concerned.

"One, I'm not a detective. Two, I'm not a psychic. I don't disagree when people call me that because they'd have a harder time with me if they knew what I really do. I see the departed. I can talk to them," I told Lindy.

"So you're a medium?"

"Not really. Mediums can sense a presence and if they're lucky communicate with it, but I see you as a flesh and blood person. Mediums don't have person-to-person conversations with the departed as we're having."

"Oh." Her gaze drifted from me for a moment. She looked lost, then distraught, as her hands came up to catch hanks of her long hair and pull them. "Then you can't help me."

But damn me, I was going to try. I couldn't cope with a nude spirit camped out in my backyard. "I might be able to, if you tell me what you need."

She crossed her wrists, wrapping the ends of her hair around her throat. "My little boy . . . I have to know what happened to Lawrence."

I frowned. The paper did not mention a child. But there could be a reason, something the police were not sharing with the public.

"He didn't leave with the police officers?"

She shook her head wildly. "No! He wasn't in the apartment. I couldn't feel him."

"Feel him?"

"I always felt him there. It was a little harder when he played outside. I had to stretch my senses farther."

"You mean you sense his physical presence?"

"Of course. Can't all parents?"

Not that I knew of. I had vague memories of my foster parents yelling through my bedroom door, "Tiffany, you stop right this minute," and not understanding how they knew what I was doing when they couldn't see me. Later in life, I learned it's intuition possessed by most parents, not an uncanny talent. Lindy meant something other than intuition.

Okay, skip it. Not important right now.

"Lawrence? He would be Lawrence. . . ?" The paper said she was single, but he could have his father's name.

"Lawrence Marchant."

"Okay. Do you have family or friends he could have gone to?"

She shook her head. "No. Nobody. We were all alone."

"Then he's probably in the state's care." I tried to give her a reassuring smile. "They'll make sure he has a good home."

I almost choked on the words. I was in and out of their shelters and went through five foster-families, till my latest foster-father made life impossible. I should have gone to my caseworker, but I just wanted out of there, fast. There are a lot of good people at Child and Family Services, but it's a state bureaucracy; too many regulations and massive caseloads can wear down most well-intentioned people. I figure I did them a favor by cutting through the red tape and leaving Utah.

"Do you think so? Perhaps they took him before I woke. Can you find out?"

I halfheartedly nodded. "If it's what you need, to know where he is, it shouldn't be hard."

Then I had to ask. "Lindy, what happened to you?"

She let her hair loose and wrung her hands together.

Until I became accustomed to it, seeing the faces of the dead was an alarming experience, because they are stuck with the expression they wore when they died. Lindy went through the physical motions of pulling on her hair and wringing her hands, as if distressed, but her expression didn't alter.

"I was taking a bath and I know I locked the front and back doors. A man came in the bathroom and went behind me. I couldn't even scream. I wanted to, but I opened my mouth and nothing came out. I gripped the sides of the tub and tried to haul myself up, and he touched me on the forehead. I barely felt it. But then it was like a . . . a jolt through my body. It took my breath away. I went under the water, just for a second, came back up and I still couldn't breathe. That's all I remember till I woke again."

I stepped closer. "What do you recall next?"

Her eyes slid away as she concentrated on a memory which could already be fading. "People there. Police. In the bathroom." Her gaze darted back to me and her tone turned indignant. "It was so embarrassing! One of the officers picked up my thong and said he wondered if his girlfriend would like one. The detective said he'd get one for his wife, but it would cut off her circulation—not that it would matter because her crotch atrophied years ago. I was stark naked in my bathtub and they joked about my underwear! And then the other officer said he'd heard on good authority if you—"

I cut in. I didn't need that much information. I kept my voice and expression neutral, although I wanted to grin at the mental picture her words evoked. "Making jokes at a crime scene is a coping mechanism. A kind of barrier they put between them and the reality of what they see and have to deal with. Your underwear was an excuse, a distraction if you like."

She stared at the ground and I hoped she hadn't lost her train of thought. But she continued: "I tried to cover myself with my hands as I got out of the tub. I yelled at them, but they took no notice, as if they didn't hear me. I tried to wrap a towel around but I couldn't seem to pick it up. I was . . . I froze. I couldn't understand what was happening. And then. . . ."

She brought her hands up to cover her eyes.

After talking to so many dead people, you would think I'd become hardened to it, but although I learned to keep my feelings to myself, their sad stories still get to me. After a while they come to terms with what happened to them, and become resigned—although I did meet a couple with a serious case of self-denial. But people like Lindy who have only just passed over—I feel so damned awful for them, for what they go through, not only losing their lives, but the frustration, disbelief and fear they experience as they come to realize they are no longer among the living.

She dropped her hands and looked me in the eyes. "They were talking about the dead woman in the tub and I realized they meant me.

"They left after a while, taking me with them. I mean . . . I watched them take my body, but *I* was still there! Then I was all alone. And then I remembered you. So I came to see you."

"How did you manage that, Lindy?"

"I walked here. It isn't far. Although it did seem to take a real long time."

Two days. She took two days to reach me.

I didn't explain how her leaving the apartment was, as far as I knew, an oddity. "I'll see what I can do. But it could take time and I can't have you waiting in my yard."

"I won't be a bother," she said quickly.

I had to be blunt. "Well, you are a bother when every time I look out the window I see you staring in."

She glanced at the yard. "I don't want to go back to the apartment. Can I stay here if I keep out of your way? If I keep out of sight?"

I closed my eyes and puffed out a quick breath. I didn't want her here, but I couldn't make her leave if she didn't want to. Compromise would work better.

The rest of the lot stretches out behind the house. I have an honest-to-god orchard back there with a pear, a couple of plums, a Bing cherry and four apple trees. Grapevines smother the back wall. The harvest is nothing special as the high altitude means a short growing season, but my neighbors are glad to come in and pick their own, and in return I get a few jams, jellies and relishes. Hoping Lindy could follow, I walked toward the orchard. "Why don't you hang out with the apple trees for now? But when I find your son, I want you gone from here, Lindy. That's the deal."

She came after me. "But where will I—"

"I don't know," I cut in. "But not here."

I'm not unsympathetic, far from it, but there have to be boundaries between the living and the dead. Their place of departure is typically their boundary, but in Lindy's case, with her ability to move about, I had to outline those boundaries for her. My backyard would *not* to be the place she lingered till she passed over.

"By the way," I added as she wandered toward the fruit trees, "the man in your apartment, what did he look like?"

She half-turned back. "I don't remember very well. He moved so fast, he was a blur. I think he had long yellow hair. Oh, and his eyes seemed to glint. I don't mean how a person's eyes can gleam in lamplight, they . . . oh, I don't know. They just looked strange."

I headed for the backdoor leading to the kitchen, acorns from the scrub oak crunching underfoot. I made a face—another oddity. The one thing the dead *never* forget is the face of their killer.

"Well?"

I poured more coffee. "It's her all right."

"And?"

"A man was in her apartment. I think he killed her, but I don't know how. She doesn't know herself. All she's interested in is her little boy." I frowned at Jack, wondering if I skipped over some of the newspaper article. "The paper *didn't* mention a child, did it?"

"If it had, I would have told you."

I got up from the table. "I'm gonna talk to Mike."

Jack went to the window in the backdoor, from where he could see Lindy. "She's a looker. Wouldn't mind wrapping myself around that."

"Now that I'd like to see," said Mel.

"Yeah, Jack," I chimed in as I headed for the stairs. "And why don't you pass me the newspaper while you're at it."

I gave Mel a conspiratorial look—we girls have to stick together. Jack glared at both of us. "I suppose you think you're funny."

"Well . . . yeah."

Dead people. They slay me.

Chapter Two

—ϒ—

Showered, clad in Levis, white long-sleeved sweater and white surgical-style tennis shoes, I headed for door, grabbing up my green corduroy jacket as I passed through the hall.

The windows of my navy-blue Subaru Forrester were thick with frost—I knew I should have put it in the garage last night. Scrape, scrape, scrape. Five minutes later, I turned off Beecher onto Second Street and headed downtown.

My cell rang. It was Colin. "Hi Tiff."

Colin is a nice guy. I met him at the court house, me on the way in, he on the way out after paying a speeding fine. We collided in the entrance, kind of rebounded, and looked each other up and down. I guess he liked what he saw as much as I did, because he apologized and invited me for coffee. That was three months ago. Colin is a gangling six-four, with fine, pale-blond hair and lazy blue-gray eyes. During my teen years, we called eyes like Col's "go-to-bed-eyes." I didn't get to that piece of furniture till our eighth date, with a little urging from me. Our relationship had progressed to the "next level" and, well, I was a happy camper.

My bones loosened a little and my voice dropped an octave. "Hi, Colin."

"Did you have a good time last night?"

"I had a great time." A nice meal at a good restaurant. A few drinks. Back to his house. His nice *empty* house. Just him and me. I call that a good night.

I got lost in the memory a little and almost drove through Gillian as she leaped out in the road. I swerved to miss her, glowering and wagging my finger. She hunched her little shoulders and backed up to the bushes from which she'd emerged.

I avoided her mother like the plague. Gillian cropped up in the conversation every time I bumped into her mom, even after three years. Listening to a mother reminisce about her dead child is really uncomfortable when the little blighter jumps out in front of your car almost every time you drive past her house.

On her way to school, Gillian had just left her front yard when some jackass plowed into her, then went on his way, leaving her dead in the street. He was still alive and she still waited to pass over.

"Tiff?"

"Uh? Oh, sorry. I was avoiding a jaywalker."

"So, when are we gonna explore the sheets in *your* bed?"

Never. "Um. I'd feel sort of uncomfortable, you know, with my aunt being here." When I met Colin, I made the mistake of telling him I lived alone, so I invented an elderly, recently bereaved aunt moving in with me. The few times Col picked me up from my house, Aunty was napping, but she was a light sleeper. I know, a pretty lame story, one which Colin would see through in a nanosecond if I let him in the house, but at the time I happened to be looking at a poster for elderly care.

"I can understand that. But she isn't there every minute of the day, is she?"

I got a familiar sinking feeling. "Pretty much. She's getting on in years, Col. She doesn't get out often."

He forced a chuckle. "You sure you don't have a husband hidden away?"

No, just two nosy roommates. The first time I invited a boyfriend back to what was then my new home, there we were getting down and dirty in my bedroom, when I saw Jack and Mel watching us over his shoulder. Killed the moment for me. Their prying had finished two prior relationships. Now it was his place or a motel, or not at all. No, we can't spend the night, an evening, an afternoon, a few hours on the bed, couch, rug in front of the fire. I didn't even dare let anyone visit for a couple of hours lest he turn amorous. Sooner rather than later, they got suspicious. They thought I was hiding something. Which I was.

As I drove past the McClusky place, the window started to fog up and I wiped at it with a piece of paper towel I kept in the car for that purpose. I therefore had an unobstructed view of Frank McClusky as he chased a small, hysterically yipping Pomeranian around the garden, while Daisy McClusky trundled after them, calling to her dog and wondering what on earth had gotten into it. I once had a conversation with Frank, during which I tried to explain how his behavior distressed his wife, but he only said how much he hated the dog while he was alive.

I told Colin I had to go as talking to him made me think about last night, and getting all gooey while driving was one hell of a distraction. He accepted this as a valid reason to end our call.

Frank and Daisy were victims of a home invasion. Frank made a break for it and was shot to death in his front yard. The felons were doing life, but they were young men. Daisy had to put up with Frank terrorizing her pooch until the men or the dog died, whichever came first.

I know people who insist the dead are all around us, although they can't tell me why the deceased linger, if there is a purpose to it, or why some remain and some pass on. I see only those who died a violent and unnatural death. They are victims of hit-and-run, innocent bystanders caught in crossfire, or the murdered, and they do not leave until their killer dies; which means there are an awful lot of them in the world just waiting for their killer to pass away, so they can move onto wherever the dead go.

Sometimes, when they finally have the opportunity, they stay here anyway. They can become so entrenched in their lifeless existence it becomes their reality. I found out the hard way. Had I bought the house a year later, I would have sensed a presence, but my ability was new and, I think, weaker back then in that respect.

I was furious when I discovered Jack and Mel in my home. Realtors are supposed to disclose a crime on the property they are marketing, and mine told me the previous owner, an elderly man, died in the house, but of natural causes. No mention of a double murder. I tried the psychic ability thing, said I detected a presence in the house, and got the usual weird look. They insisted the only death was of the previous owner, and unfortunately, my research backed that up. So I was stuck. The house was already mine. I had no legal reason to opt out. My only recourse was to sell the place.

But Jack and Mel were so damned pathetically grateful to have someone to talk to, who could tell them about the outside world and past and current events, I somehow never got to moving out.

They *were* pathetically grateful at the time. Their true nature came to the surface once they felt sure of me: sarcastic, abrasive, overbearing, demanding. But now they are more than roommates, they are family, the only family I have.

The departed lose their memories over time, so neither of my new buddies could tell me much, apart from where their earthly remains lay. In my basement, under a foot of concrete and three feet of dirt. It didn't bother me because I realized a long time ago that dead bodies are just cast off containers for what a person really was. More research turned up one Jackson Trewellyn, twenty-eight when he disappeared in the mountains above Clarion while hiking alone in 1986. Melissa Trent disappeared in 1990. Divers found her car on the bottom of Long Meadow Lake as they searched for the body of a man pulled under by the nasty little currents in there. Mel was a student at River Valley University, on her way home from her part-time evening job. She never made it. Mel is not wet, so she didn't die in the lake. Mel and Jack died in my house.

The previous owner, Frederick Coleman, died at seventy-one. He was a powerful old guy and surprised everyone who knew him when his heart gave out. I found his obituary in the library, photocopied it and showed it to

Jack and Mel, and sure enough, he did them in. So, my roommates can leave anytime they want. They just don't want to.

I should have reported the murders to the police, but what would that have accomplished? For a start, they would have dug up my basement. Mel and Jack had no grieving family to notify. And Coleman's family did not need the stigma and grief of knowing he was a murderer.

Jack and Mel could have gone on their way when Coleman died, had I not moved in the house and instantly became their best pal. If I ever move out, maybe they will too. But with me to talk to, they feel very much a part of the real world.

I returned to my hometown of Clarion, Utah, with its population of 82,000, hoping to see less of the dead than in San Francisco. I found two of them on my street and two more in my house.

Just my luck.

I haven't always seen dead people. I'd have looked sideways at anyone who told me they did, until eleven years ago. And of course, I was in a real public place, a popular little sidewalk café crowded with people on a Saturday afternoon when *it* happened. I finished my iced chai, and noticed a woman near the door of the café as I fished in my pocket for change. She stood in the heat of the sun and it burned, but she wore a gray plastic raincoat with the hood over her hair, and black rubber boots peeked from beneath her long black skirt. Another loony, but I envied her for her pale skin and the fact she didn't sweat. I sat under a big umbrella and I know my face shone pink from the heat.

I laid two dollars and some change on the table, got to my feet and walked past her, and noticed her tears. They streamed down her face, and she held her hands clenched tightly at chest level, obviously in some distress.

I went on by, but I turned my head and caught her eyes, and she stared right at me.

I couldn't help myself. I stopped and turned to her. "Are you okay?"

She looked fixedly back at me and shook her head. I guessed she was saying "no." Then I saw the big red patch on her chest just above her clenched hands, where the raincoat fell open.

She'd been shot, or stabbed.

"Oh my god!" I spun around and found every person outside the café looking at me.

"Someone call 9-1-1!" I yelled.

I turned back to the woman. "Don't worry, help is on the way." I stepped nearer to her. "Let's get you out of the sun."

It registered I didn't hear any movement behind me. I looked back over my shoulder. They still watched me, and as I looked from face to face, each dropped their eyes or turned their head the other way, or became interested in their lunch.

I couldn't believe what I saw. "Did someone call emergency services?" I asked.

Not one person glanced my way. I couldn't understand it. I know a lot of people in big cities tend to mind their business, which is why the police often have difficulty finding witnesses to a crime, but this lady stood right in front of them and they ignored her. They ignored me.

"What is wrong with you people?" I yelled.

I had never been angrier in my life. I took a couple of steps to the door of the café and stuck my head inside. "Hey! Someone call an ambulance. You got a wounded woman out here!"

Several customers looked up, startled, and two waiters went for the phone on the host's desk. I wasn't in there more than five seconds, but when I backed out, people at two of the sidewalk tables were walking away and those at another got to their feet. I glared at a couple stupid enough to meet my eyes, and one tall guy stood so fast his knees hit the table and shunted it a foot, making the umbrella tilt.

I was going to raise hell when this got over, but the woman needed my help, since nobody else seemed inclined.

When I stood in front of her again, she started moving her hands and fingers in an odd way. She was signing, which meant she was mute. I didn't know sign language.

I put my hands to her shoulders and spoke gently. "I think you should sit down."

My left hand went through her shoulder and hit the wall behind her, the brick grazing my knuckles.

My brain stopped working properly. My hand, wrist and part of my forearm were inside her body. I just stuck my arm through someone. There should be blood. She should be screaming. I should be screaming. She must be in shock and I wasn't far behind her. I heard a siren. The paramedics were a block away. I couldn't pull my arm free because then her blood would come gushing out, wouldn't it? My arm plugged the gigantic hole I made in her body.

Inches from her white face, I saw the tears on it were static, like strings of clear wax pasted to her skin.

Although my knuckles burned where they hit the wall, I didn't feel anything else other than hot Californian air. I felt nothing of substance, nothing at all. My right hand shook as I put my palm to her cheek and it started to sink in her flesh.

I guess I couldn't process any more because I blacked out. I came to in the ambulance, thinking, *I fainted? Wow! So this is what it feels like.* Laying still, my eyes closed, I thought about the reason I passed out. I knew I didn't imagine the insubstantial weeping woman. The café staff called emergency services for a wounded woman and instead carted off a loony, the same loony who yelled at their customers and talked to thin air. This loony had better keep her mouth shut if she wanted out of the emergency room.

I didn't argue when the doctor diagnosed sun stroke.

I returned to the café a week later. She still stood to the right of the entrance, her hands clenched at her chest, tears streaking her sad face.

He faced her ten feet away, and she cried because she was going to die and couldn't call out for help. She didn't know him, just a guy who popped up in front of her as she sheltered from a fierce downpour. He didn't look like he hated her, or killing her would bring him satisfaction. He just stared, and stared, and for an instant she thought he was only trying to scare her. Then he pulled the trigger.

That just came to me, the way it often does now when I see a shade for the first time. But that initial experience knocked me to my knees.

I found articles about the murder in the library. Nineteen-year-old May Wentworth worked as an assistant teacher at a private school for the deaf and blind and lived with her grandmother. They never found her killer. I learned to sign. I "talked" to her, but I couldn't help her. I looked for her killer everyplace I went. His face became an imprint in my memory.

I can't begin to tell you how many times I've wished meeting May Wentworth was an isolated incident, but it seemed I couldn't turn a corner without seeing dead people. I packed up and came back to Utah.

It's universal, I suppose: when you're in trouble you go running home. I don't know why I thought familiar surroundings and re-immersion in a culture I was once desperate to escape would make life easier. Perhaps it was the homing instinct. Clarion *was* my home. My foster homes, the foster-parents and the other kids meant nothing to me, but the city itself, the population, I understood the people and their mentality. I was older, and could see life was seldom black and white, and the gray areas in between were an acceptable compromise. I knew what to expect from life in Clarion. I felt safe, and I would not see many violently slain people in my little old hometown. Or so I thought.

She still stands outside the Sun and Bun Café. I spend a little time with May Wentworth when I go to San Francisco, but I see her in the early hours of the morning when few people are about, and I always carry my gun.

I made a long-distance call to California, to the only person I know who is like me. I met Lynn at a training gig for police consultants, where we learned about standard police procedures during various cases, so we don't get in the way and end up being more a hindrance than a help. She marched right up to me. "Hi, I'm Lynn and I see dead people." I thought, *whoa lady, you just haul your skinny little butt away from me,* until she added in a whisper, "like you do." Turned out, Lynn not only sees the shades of the dead, she's also telepathic. She picked a heap of stuff out of my mind. She knew what I was the minute I walked in the auditorium.

Lynn's talent is sporadic and she doesn't actually see shades as I do. To her they are amorphous, and there is no rhyme or reason to why she sees one here and there and not all of them, which is good for Lynn, as I can't imagine how she could cope with seeing every dead person who lingers. She doesn't pick thoughts out of every person's head, either. They come to her as flashes, and again, randomly. She calls them *insights*. And Lynn is the only other person I know who sees demons as they truly are.

"This is Lynn!" her bright voice said.

"Hi, Lynn. It's Tiff."

"Tiffany!"

I hate her calling me Tiffany. I hate my name. Really, I do. It brings to mind some bouncy, fluffy little valley girl who goes around saying *ohmygod!* all the time. Someone about as far removed from me as anyone can be.

"Yeah, well, I'm kinda in a rush, Lynn. Sorry. On my way to town. I need some answers if you have them."

Unfazed by my abruptness, Lynn kept her silence, waiting for me to speak again.

"I got a woman who walked a half-block from the scene," I went on, knowing Lynn knew I meant one of the departed. "I didn't think they could."

The silence on the end of the line lasted longer than I expected, or liked. Finally Lynn said, speaking slowly as if thinking it through, "In every aspect of life, and death, there are exceptions to the rule. I was talking to an uncooperative little spirit in a rural area of Pennsylvania, when he told me to go to hell and walked right out of the house. The last I saw of him, he was trotting down a dirt road leading to the highway. The killer was unhuman, Tiffany."

"Unhuman? You mean. . . ?"

"Yes. He was one of the Otherworldy."

A chill ran down my spine. Otherworldy. Demon.

Chapter Three

___ϒ___

The Clarion City Police Department and Fifth District Court share a big shiny building on Linden. It's all concrete and metal, with reflective glass windows which dazzle you if you drive near when the sun hits them. The acoustics in the place make voices echo and bounce around and you can't tell from which direction they come, and stiletto heels rattle like hailstones on marble. The old building on Madison, built in the 1930s, has more character but no longer has the capacity. In addition, the city jail abuts the new building, making everything more convenient for police and court alike.

A few people sat on uncomfortable wooden benches along the perimeter and more milled about. Despite my Civilian Consultant's badge, I had to cross the gargantuan entry hall and report in to the desk sergeant. I went up the escalator and took an elevator to the fourth floor, where I moseyed along the corridor, through the Squad Room and in Lieutenant Mike Warren's office.

I had worked with a number of police officers, and Mike was the only one who didn't roll his eyes when he listened to me, plus he headed up Homicide. If anyone knew about Lindy's case, he did.

Mike is a very large man, all over. He's not fat, it's mostly muscle, but he's widely built, if you know what I mean. His flat slick of wheat-colored hair sticks out over slightly prominent brows and a bulbous nose, and his reddish pockmarked skin gives him a permanently overheated look. He tends to hunch his shoulders, and he hunched over his desk as I walked in.

I plopped down in the chair facing his desk. "Favor, Mike?"

He grimaced at me as he leaned back. "Depends. . . ."

"Coralinda Marchant."

Looking interested, Mike squinched up one eye. "Lived up behind you, right? You sensing something?"

Bless him, he didn't even accentuate "sensing," saying it like a regular word where I was concerned.

Of course, the drawback of pretending to have a psychic talent is I can't repeat the lengthy conversations I have with the departed, so I couldn't always give Mike the whole story. I would get his take on the case before I told him I thought Lindy was murdered.

"I'm getting she's worried about her little boy."

He made a *harrumph* noise in his throat. "Then you're mistaken. She didn't have a child."

This stopped me cold. No child? No little boy? "Are you sure?"

He laid his hand flat on the manila folder on his blotter. "It's all here. We've talked to every resident in her apartment block over the last two days. Asking if they know of any next of kin, other relatives, or friends, is standard procedure. Nobody mentioned a son."

Trying to block out the background hum of a busy precinct, I thought hard for a second. "What about personal effects? Pictures in her wallet? Kid's stuff in the apartment?"

He shook his head side to side. "Nothing."

"I don't understand," I muttered more to myself. I gave him my best pleading look, which produced a deep sigh from him. "Could you dig a little, Mike? Pretty please? Just for me?"

He rolled his eyes before closing them, hefted a sigh. "Not officially, but if it makes you feel better, I can make a few calls."

He meant *if it will shut you up*. I smiled my thanks. "Would you? I'd really appreciate it. Lawrence Marchant, like his mother."

He got to his feet, my signal he was done with me and wanted me out his office. "Consider it done."

But I was not through. "Autopsy?"

He tapped the folder with his index finger. "We'll know more when the medical examiner is through with her, but preliminary results seem to indicate heart attack. I got someone talking to her family physician right now."

Is this a day for surprises. "But she drowned!"

"Did you get that from her?"

I pulled on my lower lip with my teeth, gave him a thoughtful look. "No."

"But you read in the paper she was found in her tub, so you jumped to the conclusion. Right?"

Crapola. Lindy didn't say she drowned. She didn't know what happened. I couldn't argue on this one. I slumped lower in the chair. "Right."

"We thought the same when we found her, but no bruising to indicate she slipped and knocked herself out, or anyone held her under. Looks like it was her heart, Tiff."

I nodded distractedly. Mike perched his butt on the edge of his desk. "It's not like you to jump to conclusions, Tiff."

"I know," I said, wriggling my shoulders. I straightened up. "But I am positive of one thing, Mike. Lindy Marchant has . . . had a son. His name is Lawrence Marchant, and he's out there somewhere."

A roll of his eyes, a light shake of the chin, and Mike forced a smile. "Okay, Tiff. I'll make those calls and get back to you. Okay?"

"Thanks, Mike." I gave him a bright smile as I got to my feet and waved my hand bye.

As I walked back through the Squad Room with its underlying aroma of male bodies and inadequately applied deodorant, someone in the far corner went *woo woo* and someone else did a lousy impression of a creaking door. I ignored them. A lot of PDs occasionally use psychics, so you'd think they would appreciate the work I did for them instead of making fun of me. But that's life in any police division; they get their fun where and when they can, because what they deal with most of the time is far from amusing.

Mike and his crew called me the Ice Queen, which had nothing to do with regal bearing or giving them the cold shoulder, because neither applied.

My silver-white hair hangs to my hips when loose, but can be a pain because of its weight, so I generally wear it in one long, fat braid. Someone told me my eyes are icy-blue and my tip-tilted nose makes me look aloof. I don't accentuate my wide mouth with lip color, as it stands out too much against my pale skin. And I am not a habitual smiler; my expression veers toward neutral.

So I was the Ice Queen. I was okay with the title. Rather they called me that to my face than repeated aloud what they said behind my back.

I sat in my Subaru, thinking.

I didn't know a thing about Lawrence, but I had no reason to ask Lindy. I thought Mike would give me some plausible reason why Lawrence was not named in the newspaper, something fairly innocuous, and I could go back home and get rid of Lindy. Did she lie to me? Shades do lie, and they can become confused. I think they cannot always distinguish between their reality, dreams or cravings when they were alive, and it becomes mixed up in their minds. Did Lindy want a child she never had? But she was newly dead; surely she had not deteriorated to such a degree in a brief time. So, either she lied to me, or the neighbors lied, or . . . I really did not want to think about a third possibility.

The alternative to Lindy lying was going to give me heartburn.

Otherwordly. Not human.

Dead people are not the only things I see.

Why can Lynn and I see demons as they really are? I have no idea. I'm pretty sure other people see normal, human men.

I gave my wrist an experimental shake, making my bracelet jingle, making sure it was there. Every tiny charm was a crucifix and each a different metal. The gold and silver made the bracelet pretty, but I bought it for the charms of metal alloys. I wore the bracelet on my right wrist and a watch with a gray steel band on my left. A stainless-steel rosary hung around my neck. We'd never had a problem with the Otherworldy in Clarion, but Lynn thought a lot of nasty stuff in other parts of the world, of the inexplicable kind, could be attributed to them. As far as I knew, at least one demon lived in Clarion, so I took precautions.

Everything I knew about the Otherworldy I got from Lynn, although *knew* was the wrong word. She spent years researching them, but it was really guesswork gathered from myth, unexplained sightings and unsolved mysteries. They can move like the wind, their hearing is acute and they are far stronger than we humans. Although they are fine with pure metals, they don't tolerate alloys well. Hence my watch and jewelry. As for the crucifixes, I just happened to like crucifix jewelry.

Lynn was trying to be ethnically sensitive, calling them the Otherworldy. It was too much of a mouthful for me; I called them demons. Not that I thought they were creatures from hell. I didn't know what they were, or where they came from. They could be aliens from outer space for all I knew. But with their slightly pointed teeth and glimmering eyes, demon seemed an apt description.

Gorge Ligori, our friendly neighborhood demon, did not know *I* knew what he was. The first time I went in his store, I couldn't decide whether I had risen to heaven or descended to hell. He is so freaking gorgeous, the prettiest man you'll ever see, almost too lovely to be a man, in fact. His long hair glows, sun-bright, golden, and on sunny days appears to reflect on his face and turn his tanned skin a lighter version of the same color. His golden brows arch enquiringly over sparking teal eyes. Lynn told me all demons are tall, but she's wrong—Gorge is about five-foot-five. Yet I see how she reached that conclusion, for although petite and slim, the picture of Gorge in my mind is of a tall, slender man, supple as a willow.

Gorge and I belonged to the Heart of Clarion Restoration Society, the nucleus of a project to revitalize the downtown area, so after our first meeting we often saw each other. I made myself treat him like a regular human being, so he did not suspect I recognized him for what he really was.

And I have to admit, if Gorge were a human he would be a pretty nice one, along with being absolutely stunning. Gorge owned and ran an antique store in downtown Clarion.

Lynn thought demons had been here a long, long time. She thought they could be the inspiration behind legends and myth: elves, vampires, even angels. She wondered if an Otherworldy being touched Lindy's spirit as it departed her body, giving it a powerful jolt. Maybe the jolt added to the spirit's range of abilities, letting Lindy move away from her place of departure. And a demon—though it would have to be a mighty powerful one—could have messed with every mind in the apartment building, making them forget Lawrence. It could have removed any trace of the child before the police got there.

I've been in the apartments; the units are similar in design. Even if Lindy went straight from the bathroom and out of the front door, she would see Lawrence's stuff had disappeared. The place was cleaned out after she left to find me.

But why would a demon murder Lindy Marchant and go to such lengths to erase all evidence of her son?

I tried to relax. If Lawrence existed, there must be records of him. Lindy had not mentioned his age, but if he went to school, there was one record. If he was younger and went to day-care while she worked, there was another. Birth-certificate. Immunization records. . . . He left his mark someplace and Mike would find it.

I tried to relax, and I couldn't. I had the nastiest feeling in my gut.

I ground my clenched fists in my eyeballs. I should get back to Lindy. I needed more information. If Lawrence was taken by Demons. . . .

Lindy quietly sat under an apple tree. The apples rotting on the ground didn't seem to bother her, and I noticed the wasps kept their distance. Jack and Mel watched me from the window in the backdoor as I walked over to her. Annoyed I didn't go inside the house first, they flapped their hands at me agitatedly. I rolled my eyes at them.

Lindy looked up at me and for the briefest of moments before her gaze sank again, although I know I imagined it, I thought I saw hope in her eyes.

I put on my cheerful face. "A friend is making some calls, so it shouldn't be long now."

I hunkered down in the grass next to her, folding my arms on my knees. In mid-November the grass was yellow and leaves almost covered the corners of the yard where they had drifted. I should get out there soon with the leaf blower. The harsh winter sun blazed down. I unzipped my jacket.

I didn't question Lindy about Lawrence, but she needed only a modicum of interest from me to start rattling on about him. I sat back and absorbed it.

Lindy and Lawrence celebrated his sixth birthday on November 9th. He attended the Saint Mary Frances Catholic School down on Monmouth Avenue. Considering she devoted her life to helping the sick and aged, I don't understand how Mary Frances' name ended up on a kid's school. In summer, Lawrence attended the summer program there while Lindy worked. He was smart, and she never had a problem getting him to finish his homework. He liked hamburgers and ice cream and all the other child-popular foods, but his favorite was Cobb salad, which I thought unusual for a little kid. He often played with the other apartment kids in the play park behind their building in the evenings and at weekends, while Lindy sat on the bench. They went to the movies and the skating rink, and went bowling a couple of times, but bowling was new to Lawrence and he didn't know yet if he liked it.

He was hospitalized with severe bronchitis when ten-months-old and spent two weeks in Primary Children's Medical Center in Salt Lake City. Their family physician was William Haskey at Clarion's Fourth Street Clinic.

Well, there should be plenty of records on this boy and hopefully I'd find some of them in Lindy's apartment. Although, according to Mike, there was nothing to indicate a child lived in the apartment, the police don't thoroughly investigate the home of a person who dies of natural causes. I meant to make a careful search and find what they missed. I needed something to get Mike off his rear end and on the trail of young Lawrence.

When she wound down I said, "I'd like a picture of him. Do you have an extra key to your place, under a mat, or a planter, or on the lintel maybe?"

She shook her head, but her wet hair didn't move; it clung to her head as if glued on.

I got to my feet. "It's okay. I can probably get in."

She rose up with me. "I'll come with you."

Damn! If Mike was right and no trace of Lawrence remained in the apartment, she would see his stuff was gone. "I don't think it's a good idea. You'll just get upset."

"I don't think I will." She looked past the trees to the apartment block. "In fact, I have a strange feeling I should be there. And I want to be surrounded by Lawrence's things."

Uh oh! I would not be able to concentrate with a hysterical spirit bugging me. I tried to stop her. "Lindy, I don't want to have to tromp over to your apartment if we need to talk."

But no, she walked away from me. She got ten paces before she stopped. "Funny. I can't go any further."

I got ahead of her. She stared at the ground. "My feet won't move."

Oh great! I didn't want her to leave my yard right then, but I definitely didn't want her stuck here. "Let's experiment, huh? Try going in another direction."

So we walked around together. Lindy could walk along the side of my house to where she stood when I first saw her, she could walk through the orchard among the trees, but she couldn't go more than twenty feet away from the house. She couldn't get near the wall.

Defeated, she folded her body to sit beneath the cherry tree.

Well, nothing I could do about it. I headed for the house.

I had no idea how to go about breaking into a building, so I called Mike, ignoring Jack and Mel for the moment.

"I won't believe nothing of Lawrence is in their apartment till I see for myself."

"Well, it's not a crime scene, so I suppose there's no harm letting you take a look. But the manager may have already cleared out the place."

"Damn! I hope not."

"I'll give him a call. Give me a few minutes."

Mike called me back five minutes later. "He hasn't got to it yet, so I let him know you'll be by."

I was relieved. If Mike had said no and I tried to barge in anyway, I would be in it deep when he found out. And I was determined to get inside Lindy's apartment, one way or another.

Chapter Four

——— ♈ ———

Jack and Mel were all around me like there were more than two of them. "Well?" from Jack. Mel hopped up and down in agitation.

So I told them about it as I went in the pantry and reached to the top shelf for a small canister I kept there. They followed me to the kitchen counter, all bated breath and widened eyes; metaphorically speaking. Skipping over the fact a little boy was missing, they zeroed in on what they considered the most intriguing aspect of Lindy's case.

"But that means. . . ." from Mel.

"Demon," Jack provided.

"Or—" Mel began, voice all fluttery.

I cut her off. "Or nothing. No vampires. No werewolves. No pixies or trolls or djinns."

"You call them demons, but you don't know what they actually are." Jack planted himself in front of me as I removed the lid from the can. "They could be anything."

"Does *Gorge* mind you calling him a demon?" Mel asked.

I did Jack the courtesy of going around him, not through him. "I don't.

Not to his face." I tightened my jaw, exasperated. "You know it's just a term I use. As Jack says, they could be anything."

Mel had an unholy fixation with Gorgeous Gorge. "Anything so cute can't be a demon."

I shook my head with irritation. "You've never met Gorge."

"I'd like to."

As if I would invite a demon in my house.

"I did see his photo in the newspaper once, and he is *cute!*"

I would never call a demon cute. Incredibly handsome. Charming. Deadly. Not to be trusted. According to Lynn, they did not blatantly lie, but could do so by omission when it suited them. And you could ask them a question and they answered in such a way that, without exactly lying, they didn't give you the truth.

Although Gorge owned his small antique shop, he didn't need a business; he didn't need the income it provided. Lynn told me demons have no interest in possessions. They were all about sensual gratification. They fed off us, off our arousal, and it gave them an incredible high. They didn't harm people they used, although they certainly could. Their victims were not hurt, they were compensated by sharing the sensations the Otherworldy themselves experienced. It could be an exquisitely rewarding relationship. Or so Lynn told me.

Lynn told me a lot about demons which later proved less than factual.

I dug in the canister and put a handful of steel filings in each pocket of my Levis. Not much in the way of protection, but I had something better as backup. If a demon killed Lindy, I was not going near her apartment unprepared.

Jack hung over my shoulder as I got my Ruger SR9 from kitchen drawer, made sure the safety was on and looked for the holster. I own a hip holster, but I prefer the angle-draw shoulder holster. The Ruger is slim, and light enough for concealed-carry, and the magazine is double stack, holding seventeen rounds. The frame is impact-resistant polymer, but the sides and barrel are stainless steel. I figured if I had to shoot a demon, and missed, I could batter it with the gun.

I didn't buy the gun with battering demons in mind. As a woman living alone, I believe in the right to defend myself. I believe in *my* right to bear arms. And because I also believe I should be able to go anywhere in my town and not fall victim to some drugged-out mugger, I have a concealed-carry permit. And although I'm no markswoman, I generally hit what I aim at, or the State of Utah would not have given me a permit.

I found the holster on the hall coat-stand, under my suede coat. Jack watched me fasten it and snug in the Ruger. "Now you're frightening me."

"Ooh! Jackie's scared to *death*!" Mel sang.

Jack shook his head. "You think you're so damn funny. You're not."

"Funnier than you, deadboy. I can tell a joke we haven't heard like a million times."

"Really?" Jack's hands went to his hips. "Let me have it."

Mel's head jutted forward. "If only I could. I'd let you have it . . . right where it hurts."

Jack beckoned with crooked fingers. "Bring it on, baby."

As they argued, I crept past them and out of the backdoor.

A ten-foot-high redbrick wall surrounds my orchard on three sides, which makes the place kind of stick out, because no other properties in the area have high walls. A few old maple and sycamore rear up behind the wall and beyond them the apartment complex raises its head.

It was not here when I moved in. Just a matted, humpy old field and a few trees. The way land was at a premium in the area, I should have known someone would build eventually.

A tall wrought-iron gate bisects my wall. I used to imagine previous owners of my house taking their dogs through there for their morning walk among the trees, then across the field. I went that route myself to reach a small, family owned corner-store called Marvin's Mart until it fell victim to the apartment complex.

I started off in the dusk. The woods were not very deep and the lamps from the street ahead penetrated through the trees. The air was crisp and cold, permeated by wood smoke, and I would have seen a lot more stars if not for the glow from Clarion behind me. Leaves crunched under my feet; one more good wind and those remaining on the trees would come down. The leaves turned early this year and looked crispier, and I wondered if the past summer's drought had something to do with that.

In a couple of minutes, I was standing on the curb, looking across the street at the three-story apartment complex.

To give them their due, whoever designed the complex tried to make it blend in with the area and the old east bench homes. Built of honey-colored brick with steeply pitched slate roofs, oak doors and window frames, it looks older than it actually is. The main block faces east, with a wing extending at each end, surrounding a beautiful expanse of lawn trisected by cobblestone paths. The sidewalks surrounding the entire complex are likewise cobblestone. At each corner, where the wings join the main block, an arched passage goes through to the rear of the complex.

Borders of shrubs and annuals had been tidied up and mulched for the winter, but I remembered how pretty they looked in spring, summer and early fall. I waited for two cars to drive past, then crossed the street.

As is often the case, the manager's apartment is on the ground floor just off the main entrance. The manager, a small, balding man, was not at all interested in me or why I wanted to get inside Lindy's apartment. Yes, Lieutenant Warren called him and here was the key. He kept looking back over his shoulder at his TV as he spoke to me, and the door shut in my face before I took more than one step back.

I went outside and through one of the passages to the back. I looked over a nice little play area for the kids and a fenced-in swimming pool, now covered, the gates locked. I wanted to get to Lindy's apartment from the rear, to see if I could spot anything odd on the backstairs going up.

The top floor apartments boast wrought iron balconies. A lot of them had plastic chairs, a potted plant or two. Lindy's balcony was bare.

I used the key, stepped inside, and with my left hand searched the wall for a light switch. Strip lighting on the ceiling and recessed globes above the cabinets illuminated the kitchen in stark detail. Small, but very nice, with plenty of oak cabinets going right up to the ceiling, a built-in gas stove near the sink, dishwasher, trash compacter, and a free-standing refrigerator against the outside wall. The kitchen was very neat, with only a microwave, a few canisters, a can opener, a coffee maker, and a jug containing utensils precisely arrayed on the single counter. The dishes were still in the dishwasher—clean. A small oval antique dining table with two chairs just managed to fit in near the backdoor.

An arch gave into the living space. This room was a good size. A couch and matching armchair in soft beige leather. A small antique buffet with a few tasteful knickknacks. A forty-two-inch plasma TV on a small unit. An end-table between the chair and couch. A small antique roll-top desk. A couple of very nice reproduction Constable prints on the walls.

The air was stuffy and warm, the scent of rose potpourri cloying. I looked inside the home entertainment unit and sorted through a few DVDs. None of them were for kids. Opening up the desk, I found utility bills bound with rubber bands, notepaper, envelopes and various other documents, but none of them had anything to do with a little boy named Lawrence Marchant.

A short hall went from the front door past the living room to the bedrooms and bathroom. The bathroom was fairly basic with tub and showerhead, sink, toilet, medicine cabinet over the sink, and the counters were a pale green marble which almost matched the tiled floor in color. Unused rose and honeysuckle candles sat in the windowsill. I checked the cabinet and found the usual self-medicating pharmaceuticals and feminine hygiene products. No kiddie bubble baths or Disney toothbrushes. No bath toys lined up on the rim of the tub. The tub was mildly scummy and a bottle of baby oil had tipped over to leave an oily trail down the inside. A few items of clothing draped a small stool, with Lindy's thong on top of the pile.

I went in her bedroom. Pretty, with a bright-yellow comforter on the queen-sized bed, and matching curtains. A yellow and cream rag-rug by the bed. A big old oak ladies wardrobe which matched the oak dressing-table, both antique pieces. Hair products and cosmetics littered the dressing-table's French-polished top. Clothes crammed the wardrobe, with shoes sitting in a row along the floor of it. More clothes lay crumpled on an overstuffed yellow and white paisley armchair in one corner of the room.

Lawrence was taking a nap in his room. I opened the door to the second bedroom and looked in. A blue and green plaid spread on the twin bed. Matching drapes were closed over the window. A small bedside unit with a blue-shaded lamp. A built-in closet, the doors wide open to show it was empty. Nothing else. The room looked like a seldom used guest bedroom fitted out with the bare necessities, not the den of a little boy.

I saw a *lot* of little holes in the wall, about the size a tack makes. Pictures? There were none now. Perhaps the holes were made before Lindy moved in, or maybe she had pictures up at one time and took them down. I had no cause to think a child's drawings once covered the walls. I checked under the bed and in the bedside unit.

It was a nice apartment, and I couldn't help but compare it to my cluttered house with its dark living room and antiquated fittings, although the apartment must cost a pretty penny to lease.

After my preliminary look through, I started in earnest. I looked in every drawer, every closet, every cupboard.

Did not find a thing.

One thing struck me as odd: no photos, not even of Lindy.

If anyone cleaned the place of all traces of Lawrence, they did a thorough job. I sat on the couch for a moment, trying to think of anyplace I could have missed.

It was dark out and time for me to get back home. I was not going to find anything.

But as I walked through the kitchen, I noticed all the magnets on the fridge. A lot of them. Most of them were free giveaways from utility companies, plumbers, that type. Some of them were scuffed on the surface as if they had been handled a lot. But there were a whole heap of little ones, the kind out of which you make poetry or witty saying. *Hugs, Heart, Children, Love, Warm, Mommy, Cuddles, Baby,* to name a few. I moved some, putting them in a straight line across the fridge: *Children leave imprints on your heart.* I read that somewhere.

Why would a childless woman have those on her fridge?

I opened up the freezer section, then the refrigerator, but nothing inside particularly looked like kid's food. Just your basics.

Then I saw the edge of a piece of paper under the fridge.

I bent and tried to pull it free, but it was stuck on something. Gripping the sides of the fridge, I pulled one way then the other, walking it along the kitchen floor. It was a small unit and as I said, I'm a big girl; it moved easily. I uncovered dust balls, a paperclip and *there!*

A child's drawing done in Crayola. A tall building. A tree with a woman and a man beneath? Or a boy and a girl? Maybe a mother and her little boy? And another person near the building. And on the bottom in large, untidy scrawl: *lawrence.*

The tall figure had long yellow hair. The man who came in Lindy's bathroom and touched her? Did he watch them while Lawrence played outside?

I folded it and put it in a pocket. As I did, I heard a noise behind me, a bare whisper. I spun to face the room.

He was almost on me, coming at incredible speed, his long hair streaming behind him, black streaked with blood-red, his long leather coat whipping back. His eyes were a bright sparkling green in a sharply chiseled face. And that's all I had time to see before he leaped at me.

I knew what he was.

I brought my hand out my pocket and flung steel in his face.

He stopped like he'd been pole-axed, hands clawing at his face. The filings worked; they were already burrowing in his skin and I smelled charred flesh.

I didn't wait to see any more. Leaving the lights blazing in the apartment, I was through the backdoor and hurtling down the stair. Demons heal quickly and the filings would be just a minor annoyance once he got over the shock. And demons were fast. Heart pounding, I took the steps two at a time.

I jumped the last five steps and hit the ground with an impact which sent pain shrieking up through my ankles and shins. I ignored it and charged through the passage and across the grass, reaching under my jacket to pull the Ruger. I didn't look back; I concentrated on running.

Something dug in my calf and I pitched on my face, all the air knocked out of me. The pistol flew out of my hand. He had me, he had hold of my leg. His nails punched through denim and bit in my flesh. I wanted to scream but didn't have the breath.

I stopped trying to move and lay passively as I waited to get air back in my lungs. The grip on my right calf didn't let up, but I felt his other hand on the inside of my thigh. It slowly slid up my leg. An odor of charred flesh and cinnamon emanated from him.

I gasped in air. Rolling, I brought my left leg up and slammed my foot in the side of his head. He barely registered the blow, his head jogging over just a little. He let go of my calf, but both his hands immediately clamped on my thighs. As I lay on my back, looking at him, he smiled, a nasty little grin which showed the pointed ends of his teeth.

His black-red hair dripped over his shoulders like molten lava and his eyes glinted emerald as he looked in mine. Oh god, he was beautiful. His fingers, hot, strong and supple, massaged the inside of my thighs. I raised my hand to touch his face. He dipped his head to let me stroke his cheek. His skin was like silk. My lips parted in invitation as I lifted my head.

I thought of Lawrence.

I let my head fall back to the damp grass and tried to appear relaxed as I smiled into his face. He smiled back, a dreamy, possessive expression. I looked at the end of his nose, not his eyes. *You don't look in a demon's eyes.* His hands slid up my thighs until his thumbs brushed my groin through the denim. With a little shudder, I drew a hissing breath through my teeth—it felt good, better than it should. I grit my teeth and inched my hand nearer my pocket.

His right hand moved to my waist and up to the underside of my right breast, while the thumb of the other slowly stroked me. I wanted him, badly. My hips writhed in rhythm with the movement of his fingers, the soft strokes and gentle nips. His power rolled over me, in my blood and bones, in the sweetness of a demon's caress.

But I wasn't some unsuspecting woman who didn't know what had its hands on her. Fear and adrenaline can override a demon's mojo. And I had an ally, sixteen-year-old Tiff, who swore no man would ever again use her body against her will. The world came back into focus; I smiled crazily through clenched teeth, sat up and slammed my wrist against the side of his face. He screamed as the charms on my bracelet sizzled on his skin and I tossed another handful of steel right in his gaping mouth.

I heard him coming after me as I reached the street.

A car drove along the street, and as I jumped over the curb and on the road, it slowed and stopped. The passenger door opened. The driver twisted in his seat, looking back at me. In the car's dome-light I saw his hand wildly beckoning.

I do not make a habit of getting in a stranger's car, but I swear I thought it was some guy passing by who saw me pelting along and the man coming after me, and wanted to help.

I must have been out of my mind.

I dashed the few feet to the car and threw myself in the passenger seat. The car moved off before I could get the door shut, so for a few seconds I struggled to close it. The driver put his foot down, flooring it, and the car sped up. Gasping, I looked back through the rear window.

Not a thing. The demon was not coming after us.

I shuddered and turned back to the driver.

Long silken hair like a solid sheet of gold slithered over his shoulders. Gold-tinted skin. Arching golden eyebrows and arching cheekbones. Bright sapphire eyes tilted at the corners. A long narrow nose and mobile mouth. Which smiled at me.

Damn.

"Hello, Tiff. My name is Caesar and I'm very pleased to meet you. Very pleased indeed."

Good Lord, even his voice was beautiful.

I tried a smile, but I think it ended up a grimace. "I don't suppose you'd stop and let me out?"

He chuckled. "After all the trouble you put my partner through? I don't think so." His smile became a sneer. "Get comfortable. We have a long drive ahead of us."

"Where are you taking me?"

"Does it matter?" He briefly took his eyes off the road to leer at me. "We will have *such* a good time."

That did it. No demon would put his hands on me again. I groped in my right pocket.

He kept his eyes on the road and the smile on his face. "I'll probably crash the car if you throw that in my face."

I threw the handful at his cat's eyes.

Chapter Five

I hobbled home. My hip was on fire and I probably had road burn all down my right leg. My right cheek was scraped and bruised and my wrist, where I stupidly slammed it down to try to break my fall, could be badly sprained. My calf stung where the black-haired demon stuck his nails in me.

When the car careened across the road, I got the door open and rolled out. It disappeared down the street, weaving back and forth all over the place and not decreasing speed for a moment.

Must have hurt the bastard. Good.

I wended through the trees with the Ruger in my hand. I didn't know whether a bullet could kill a demon, but I hoped it would hurt him. Going back and rooting in the shrubbery till I found my pistol took everything I had in me. Instinct screamed at me the entire time: *get out of here!* But I couldn't leave it for some kid to find.

I ran the last few feet to the backdoor, slammed through it and slammed it shut behind me. I threw the deadbolt then went through to the front hall and made sure the door was locked. Then back to the kitchen to sink on a chair.

"You look like shit," from Jack.

Like I don't know. I couldn't even come up with a retort. I was tired and sore and winded. I slid the safety back on the Ruger and laid it on the table, then let my head fall on my crossed arms. In a peculiar state of combined exhaustion and exhilaration, I could have fallen asleep then and there, except my heart went a mile a minute and my throat felt like it wanted to close up. I wanted to cry with relief because I made it back home.

I couldn't go to the police. What would I say? *Oh, by the way, there are demons in Clarion, have been all along. I'm pretty sure they're involved in Lawrence's disappearance. And, oh yeah, they're nasty, evil sonsofbitches.*

I hauled myself upright and went through the house with my canister of metal filings, sprinkling a smidgen on every window ledge and on the floor at the base of front and back doors. Then I put some in the cold, empty fireplaces in the living room and my bedroom.

I let the kitchen blinds down, something I did not as a habit bother with. I was majorly freaked.

No way could I get out of telling Jack and Mel what happened, so I spent the next happy fifteen minutes doing so. Then I stripped in the bathroom and looked myself over.

My hip and leg looked like someone used a cheese grater on them, and ugly bruises marked me like decaying blossom. What felt like punctures on my calf were little more than indentations, but who knew what lurked under a demon's fingernails, so I liberally doused them with antiseptic. My wrist hurt like hell, so I taped it with a stretchy surgical bandage.

I got in bed. I didn't think I would sleep. I was right

I staggered downstairs to the kitchen, my eyes puffy from lack of sleep.

"And don't you look bright and chipper," Jack drawled.

I snarled at him, and fumbled in the cabinet for coffee. I managed to knock three packets on the counter and one on the floor, where it spilled open. What a waste of Columbian.

"And her coordination is . . . well, she doesn't have any," Mel said.

Sometimes I hate my roommates.

Jack went to the backdoor. He stood looking through the side window, hands clasped behind his back. He swayed back and forth on his heels. "It's a beautiful day in the neighborhood," he chirped.

"Shut it, Jackson."

Mel joined him so they stood shoulder to shoulder. "A demon in Lindy's apartment? Why was he there?"

Yes. Why? I stepped over the spilled coffee to dump some of the good stuff in the coffeemaker. I'd need a full pot to get me up and moving.

But move *where*? Where to start? My mind buzzed with questions for which I had no answer. Why was the black-haired demon in Lindy's apartment? Why attack me? How did Caesar know my name? Was Caesar the yellow-haired man who touched Lindy as she struggled in her bathtub? I hung over the coffeemaker, one hand braced on the counter as I rubbed at my forehead with the other. What had I got myself into?

My head hurt.

I collapsed in a chair and held my face in my cupped hands. I had to tell Lindy something pretty soon and it would cause her more grief than she deserved. As if she hadn't already been through enough.

The phone rang. I leaned back far enough to see Caller ID, then swung out of the chair to grab the phone. "Mike?"

"Tiff? We got a situation in Salt Lake. I want you down there."

Just like that, I was wide awake. "What going on?"

"Someone went berserk in the 45th Street Mall. Gunned down fifteen people, four of them dead."

"So—I'm filling in the blanks here, Mike—you have it under control or you wouldn't call a civilian to the scene, so why do you need me?" I frowned at the phone. "Can any of the wounded identify the shooter?"

"Several escapees confirmed the shooter wore a mask," Mike replied. "He could still be inside. The mall was open twenty minutes, so only a couple hundred people in there, half of them mall employees. Nearly everyone managed to get out while he was still on a rampage. He was still shooting when SWAT secured the perimeter. The shooting stopped when we went in. We found people hiding all over the place. We brought out the casualties, but now we got sixteen people in the food court and he could be one of them. He only had to take off his mask. . . ."

That sounded ugly. I was not thinking of my own safety, but of fifteen innocent people penned in the mall with a killer who must be undergoing a mental episode or something.

"I thought as the scene is fresh, you might pick something up," Mike continued.

Mike thought as well as receiving messages from the recently dead, I saw ethereal images of violent criminal acts which resulted in death, like imprints on the atmosphere. And he worked that out all by himself. Clever man. I hoped I never had to disabuse him of the notion.

"Okay, I'm in. Am I driving up with you?"

"We'll take a copter. Meet me on the roof in fifteen."

Fifteen minutes? I groaned as the coffeemaker cheerily announced a full pot of perfectly brewed coffee.

"You okay, Tiff?"

"I'm fine," I snapped. I took in a breath. "Just tired, Mike. I'll be there."

I dropped the phone in the cradle and gave the coffeemaker an evil look.

Mel stood at my shoulder, bouncing on the balls of her feet. "What, what, what?"

I gave her and Jack an abbreviated version as I got my biggest travel mug from cabinet above the stove. Of course this wasn't enough for either of them—they wanted me to solve the case without leaving the house. I firmed my jaw and tried to be patient, but I was not in the mood. When I stopped talking and just plain glared, they finally quit, moodily going to the west windows, leaving me in peace. It would not last.

I filled the mug with coffee and sipped it black and scalding as I went upstairs to my bedroom. Shucking out of my robe, I kicked my slippers across the room, then pulled the first pair of jeans my hand fell on from the closet. One knee was ripped, but hey, it's fashionable, isn't it? A winter-weight T-shirt. *Boots, boots, where are my boots?*

I sat on the edge of the bed and organized my thoughts. *If you're wearing boots, you need socks, Tiff.* One pair of socks coming right up.

More or less decently clad, I clomped down the stairs, took my green jacket and matching scarf off the coat-rack, tucked my Ruger in my back pocket, and headed out.

I looked up at the snowcapped peaks which surround Clarion, breathing in air with more than a nip to it. I pulled my collar up around my neck. The first snowfall, quickly come and gone, nonetheless surprised everyone when it arrived in mid-October, and now the gray sky seemed to hang low. More snow would fall in the next forty-eight hours. I hoped we were not going to have another bad winter. The Subaru needed new tires, but I couldn't afford them.

The advantage of living in a small city is getting anywhere fast takes practically no time at all. Seven minutes after Mike called, I was dressed and running the electric toothbrush over my teeth. A couple of minutes later and I backed the Subaru from the garage, and after a six minute drive I pounded up the steps of the Court House, clutching my travel mug of coffee like only death could separate us.

I headed for the desk sergeant, but she saw me coming and pointed to the escalator, so I veered across the hall, trotting between groups of people who gave me funny looks, as if they thought I had a nerve, haring madly through such hallowed ground. I went up the escalator two steps at a time. A couple of patrolmen held an elevator for me at the top.

Wow. Did I feel special.

I still had to slog up a flight of steps to get to the roof. The pilot fired up the copter when he saw me step on the flattop. Mike was already belted in and waiting for me. He leaned to give me a hand, and hauled me inside.

I fastened the seatbelt and settled back. "Can you get those sixteen people near where someone died?"

The copter juddered a little and lifted off. "Half the victims were shot in the stores around the food court."

We didn't talk for a while. I sipped and watched the landscape sweeping beneath us. Mike finally broke the silence. "Your Coralinda had a damaged heart. From the fluid around her lungs and an enlarged liver, it looks like heart failure was an ongoing condition for quite some time. She probably had numerous minor heart attacks and didn't realize what they were."

I frowned. "But she was so young. How could she have heart problems?"

"The usual culprits: high blood pressure and cholesterol off the charts. Heredity was likely a factor."

I mulled it over. So Lindy had a damaged heart and died of it, but a heart attack can be induced. I couldn't dismiss what she told me, the man who touched her on her forehead, the jolt to her body. She lingered, I saw her, and that only happened with the violently slain. She was murdered.

He *had* to be a demon—the one who attacked me in Lindy's apartment? No, not the same guy; her attacker had yellow hair. Caesar? Recalling how he looked me over in the car, I shuddered.

"Tiff?"

I blinked. "What did you find out about Lawrence?"

Mike's voice went gruff, which meant he was embarrassed. "I got a lot on my plate, Tiff. I passed it onto Royal Mortensen. You can talk to him when we get back."

"A little boy is missing and you *passed it on*?" I growled. "And who is Royal Mortensen?"

"The new guy. Transferred in from San Antonio."

"San Antonio to *Utah*? Whose bad side did *he* get on?"

Mike glared at me. "It was voluntary. Roy's record is impeccable."

"When did he make detective?"

"Six years ago. He served two years in New York City, one in Seattle, three in San Antonio. Two commendations. He's a good guy, Tiff."

I made a derogatory noise in my throat. Why would a career cop want to leave the hustle and bustle of a big city for little old Clarion, where nothing much happened? Well, not ordinarily. "Sounds like he didn't stay too long in one place. I give him six months."

I pulled the folded drawing out my pocket and handed it to him

"What's this?" he asked as he unfolded it. Next minute: "Where did you get it?"

"Under the fridge. Oh, and your guys didn't notice the refrigerator magnets either."

He stared at it a good long time.

He finally looked up. "Refrigerator magnets?"

"The type where each is a different word and you put together poetry or sayings. These particular ones were stuff like *Mommy, cuddles, baby, hugs,* etcetera."

His mouth became a thin line. "Tiff, we had no reason to think a child lived there, and nothing obvious to clue us in on it."

"But you didn't go back and check after I told you about Lawrence," I pointed out relentlessly.

Mike sighed and fished in a pocket for a plastic bag, carefully inserted the drawing, and sealed it.

"You better not give me a hard time over contaminating evidence, either."

But he didn't. For the rest of the brief flight he looked out of the window, brow knotted, and ignored me.

Chapter Six

———♈———

The copter took us over the Wasatch Range. To the north of us, the Northfork Road from Clarion wound down Fork Canyon to the Salt Lake Valley. We cleared Mount Lomond and dropped to a lower altitude, and followed Interstate 15 to Salt Lake City. The smaller cities along the path of I-15 are so close together, they could be one vast metropolis, but when you near Salt Lake you know it; pollution is a dirty orange-brown smudge over the city.

The copter set down on the mall's parking lot, which was cordoned off. A gaggle of reporters hung over the ropes. I turned up my collar and ducked my head as I hopped to the tarmac. Bulbs popped in an explosion of light, but we were around the copter and headed inside the mall, and I didn't think they got a good picture of any of us.

The mall was empty and eerily silent, the only sound the creak of police-issue leather shoes and holsters. Dazzled by the reporter's flashbulbs, the place seemed darker than it should as my eyes tried to adjust. We walked down a long corridor to get to the food court. Every store was lit up, but empty, sending out glittering temptation for shoppers who would not be coming in.

Sixteen people of varying ages and both sexes sat on plastic chairs at plastic tables in the food court. Some held cups of coffee or soda. SWAT stood around the perimeter. I didn't give them more than a quick glance; I looked around at the stores.

I immediately spotted them. Obviously bewildered, a middle-aged woman with a thick waist and short, curly brown hair, and a brown-haired teen girl, maybe fifteen-years-old, stood just inside a teen boutique. The girl had a chest wound which bled a lot before she died. A tacky red swath of browning blood ran from just inside the entrance out into the food court.

Mike talked to a SWAT guy. He nodded at the man and walked over to me. "We found his arsenal and mask where he dumped them."

"He could still be out there."

Mike looked at the tired-looking people at the tables. "If he is, we'll find him, but he could be one of them. As a precaution, we frisked them, told them it's standard procedure. It was cursory, but we would have found a weapon."

He laid his hand on my shoulder. "Anything here you can use?"

I eyed the woman and girl. "Oh, yes."

I walked over to them. Mike stayed where he was, letting me do my thing without interference.

They watched me coming and the way I looked right at them, and straightened up. The woman wore an expression of utter terror. The girl's eyes were glazed, her mouth slightly open as if in a tiny *pop.* She was already in shock when she died. Mother and daughter?

He shot the woman first. He pulled her away from her daughter, out to the food court, pushed her to the ground and shot her in the back of the head. He went back in for the girl. She stood in the boutique with her mouth open, not believing what she saw. He shot her in the chest, and when she crumpled, dragged her out to die beside her mother. Both died just outside the store, but their shades could evidently go back inside if they wanted to. The killer wore a ski-mask, and his thin mouth smiled through the slit as he slaughtered two innocent people. I closed my eyes and sucked in several deep breaths before I could continue.

I stopped just inside the entrance, standing clear of the blood trail and shielded from outside view by a display of Prom dresses.

"Can you see us?" the woman asked.

I nodded. They needed time to ask their questions and adjust to the fact I *could* see them.

The teen still clutched a pair of bloodstained, embroidered jeans with a price tag. I've always found it interesting how the dead keep what they held when they died, like my friend Brenda Lithgow, who stands in downtown Clarion with her loaded shopping cart.

With fingers clenched in the material, the girl hugged the jeans to her chest. "We thought they were ignoring us, but they're not, are they."

I shook my head.

The mother's voice was almost a wail. "We can't get out!"

"You'll get out, but not for a while."

As if she didn't hear me, she went on, "We tried, but we can't leave the food court!"

The girl looked out at the court. "I keep telling her we're dead. She won't listen."

I stuck my hands in my pants pockets and explained everything to them, but although the teen had already come to terms with what happened to her and her mom, the woman couldn't accept the truth. So I stepped up to them and did the one thing which always convinces the dead: I stroked my hand through the woman's shoulder. Then I did the same to the teen.

They moved closer together. They wanted to cry, but they no longer possessed the ability. They wanted to hold each other, but it was no longer an option. For the umpteenth time, I wished I could say something to make it all better, but I couldn't. They were dead.

They looked at my hand dumbly. I looked back at Mike over my shoulder. He made a discrete hurry-up motion with one hand.

I spoke to the teen: "What's your name?"

"Amy."

"And you?" I asked the mom.

"June Pollock. Amy and I . . . ." Slapping one hand over her mouth, she lost it again.

Time was a ticking. I needed to identify the killer so Mike and SLCPD could get everyone out of the mall. I would have to come back and talk to June and Amy later, and I had to find the other two deceased people and talk to them. I gestured at mom and daughter. "Can you tell me who did this to you?"

June gulped. She lifted one hand and pointed at the food court. "Him."

I turned to see the food court. "Describe him."

"He's sitting between a tall, bald old man and a little boy. He's wearing a navy blazer and black slacks. Some kind of nametag on his lapel."

I spotted him. A short man, in his late twenties maybe, slicked back black hair and a pale face. He looked like a mall employee.

Yeah. You can look pale, buddy. You're not going home a free man.

"Thank you. I'm going to talk to the police officers in charge and they'll take care of him."

Now the fun would begin. Mike had only my word this guy was the killer, but at least he had someplace to start. The hardest part would be persuading Salt Lake City PD to take the man into custody. If Mike could do that, SLCPD would follow procedure by scouring the mall and the accused for evidence, and looking at his background. I'd known Mike to tuck a suspect away in a holding cell, wear him down, try to brow-beat a confession out of him, but Mike didn't run this case. But I was betting evidence nailed this bastard.

Not all the cases on which I worked had a successful conclusion. The word of a person who delves in the paranormal is not respected, and of course, seldom believed by people in general, so their participation is rarely mentioned. Imagine the field-day a defense attorney would have with a psychic on the witness stand. Good hard evidence wins a case. One case in Nevada, the accused walked owing to a seemingly infallible alibi. I knew he did it, but the police had no proof. But I felt positive about this case—forensics would find all kinds of nifty little incriminating things on this man's body.

"And him," a young voice said from behind me.

I spun back to Amy. Another one? There were two of them? "Where?"

She lifted her chin and jerked it. "Short brown hair, camouflage jacket, black Levis, backpack on the ground by his feet."

Oookay! I was not even going to look at the guy directly. "I'm going to talk to the police now," I told them, "but I will be back."

The mother's tone was bitter. "We understand. You have to take care of the living."

I ambled back to Mike trying to appear casual. Every eye in the food court tracked me. They wondered about me, why I was here.

I walked past Mike and he fell in behind me. I stopped when we got to the far side of the food court. He came in close and ducked his head to bring it near mine. I described the killers and told him where they sat.

Mike put a hand on my shoulder and gave me a little push. "You head outside. We'll take care of this."

I didn't argue. I headed back the way I came in. I heard a voice behind me. "I don't want to alarm you, but we think the perpetrators are still in the mall. We're going to escort you out one at a time. Please remain seated until two officers come for you. . . ." The voice faded as I drew away from the food court. I exited the mall and stood near the door.

Before long, they came out one at a time, each escorted by a couple of officers or members of SWAT. They were separating the civilians as if it were standard procedure, so they could take care of the suspects without risking a confrontation and endangering the others.

The press had been herded away and I understood why. One shout, one stupid remark or question could easily jeopardize the operation.

The mall employee came out fifth, but two SWAT swooped in and steered him behind the waiting bus. The brown-haired guy was twelfth. He must have suspected something.

He dropped his backpack and bent over to pick it up. Next thing I knew, he held me by the upper arm, the blade of a knife pressed in my neck, one of those small jackknifes which don't take up much space in a pocket. I understood how the police missed it when they patted him down.

The two SWAT who accompanied him dropped to one knee and held their pistols steady on him. He jerked on my arms and stepped behind me, keeping the knife blade at the side of my throat.

My day was getting better and better.

He backed inside the entrance of the mall, towing me with him. Before we got more than fifteen feet, he took us through a mall office door. He slammed the door shut, pushing me inside the office, where I stopped between two desks.

The place didn't have any windows. Another door led off to god-knows-where.

He waved his little knife at me. "Over there against the wall, bitch!"

I edged over to the wall and a clear space with no desks or other furniture against it.

I was pissed and also very, very frightened.

A hostage situation is never predictable. The felon is as scared as his captives. Even as he makes demands, he knows the cops will get him in the end. The odds are stacked too high against him. He starts to think he has nothing to lose, which is when he's most dangerous.

This guy was scared almost out of his pants. He stood against the door, trying to listen through it, waving the knife about in one hand while he gnawed at a hangnail on the other. He didn't pay much attention to me. I was a female hostage and he toted a weapon, right?

He jumped back. Maybe he decided standing near the door was not such a good idea. Maybe the cops would shoot through it. I could see him losing it soon.

"They'll be phoning in soon, asking for your terms?" I said amicably.

"Shut up!" he hissed.

"What are you going to ask for?" I continued as if he hadn't spoken.

He moved to stand in front of me and pointed the knife at my face. "I said, *shut up!*"

I shrugged. "Just trying to help. You should ask for a copter to the airport, then a jet. A jet is awful hard to stop and can take you anyplace in the world. Now a car, on the other hand. . . ."

He was getting mad now. I held up one hand placatingly, palm out.

"You don't want to hurt me. Lose your bargaining power. Nothing to stop them blasting their way in here if I'm dead."

He looked at the hand I held up. I brought up the Ruger and put it point to point on the blade.

I gave him a brittle smile. "Mine's bigger than yours and it goes bang."

He got a scared-rabbit look, but then his hand slowly dropped and a little spark in his eyes told me he thought about lunging at me. My hand followed his down. I made my face and voice chill. "Drop it!"

The knife clattered on the floor. I stepped back.

For a moment, all kinds of things went through my mind. Did he feel the same fear as his victims as he held his gun on them, just before he fired? How many of the dead did he kill? If I pulled my trigger, a few less ghosts would wander the mall.

We were alone. Only the two of us would know I didn't fire in self-defense. And he wouldn't be telling anyone.

The door burst open. I jumped and the Ruger wobbled in my hand. "Okay, we'll take it from here," Mike said.

I am not some badass with nerves of steel. I was terrified the whole time.

Mike was furious with me, but I shrugged it off. Did he really think I would let someone stab me when I had a gun and knew how to use it?

When we got back to Clarion, after I gave my statement, he bundled me in my car with orders to go home and stay put for a couple of days.

Another case over. Another paycheck. And four people who must linger in a mall, unseen, unheard, until their killers died.

And I don't know what I would have done if Mike hadn't come through the door when he did.

Chapter Seven

—♈—

"Um, you have a visitor," Mel said.

"He's on the porch," Jack supplied.

I eyed them. They did not look any happier than I. They looked nervous. But then, they always look nervous.

I backed to one of the narrow windows either side of the front door and peeped out.

Holy. . . ! He leaned on the wall in profile, but there was no mistaking Caesar, his long sheet of golden hair pushed back over his shoulders, slightly iridescent golden skin. He stood with hands in the pockets of a tan, calf-length, butter-soft leather duster, with a pale-tan silk shirt beneath and brown suede pants which couldn't get any tighter if they tried. The shirt opened at the neck and gold glinted at his throat. Gold in his ears too: a long earring in the shape of a feather almost touched his shoulder. He turned his head to me and smiled, his blue sapphire eyes gleaming beneath thin golden eyebrows.

He was something to behold.

I heard him through the thick walls and storm windows, clear as if he stood next to me. "Come out, come out, wherever you are!" he sing-songed.

I backed from the glass and there he was looking through it.

"Please," he said, and his voice whispered through my bones.

Spirits, demons—could no one wait till I had my morning coffee?

I stalked back to the kitchen and turned on the radio, loud. KXGB cooperated by blasting out Metallica's *Sandman*. Oldie but goodie. I hiked the volume up louder and flipped on the coffeemaker.

Jack and Mel stood side by side next the backdoor. "What are you going to do?" Jack asked.

I pulled a clean mug from cupboard. "I have absolutely no idea." I paused. "Amend that. I'm going to call the cops. I found a stranger on my porch. I told him to leave but he refused. I'm afraid to go out and confront him. If *I* call the cops, there'll be half a dozen squad cars here in less than ten minutes."

"The way he can move, he'll be gone before they pull up," Jack said.

I thought it over. True. Plus, maybe he didn't care if he stirred up trouble. Maybe he'd hurt them. His pal seemed to enjoy hurting me.

So, calling the cops was not one of my better ideas.

Figuring if I could hear him, he could hear me, I turned down the radio, plucked up the phone, dialed the time and temp line and made my *report* to the tinny voice.

I went back to the front door and yelled through it. "I just called the police."

He appeared at the narrow glass pane again. "I only want to talk."

"Yeah, well, make an appointment."

Never taking his eyes off me, he lifted his hands to shoulder height, backed across the porch and down the steps. He smiled, just slightly. I watched him till he passed the Henderson's place and disappeared from sight.

I opened the door and walked out on the porch.

I knew demons could really move, but not how fast. Pressing his body against mine, he pinned me to the wall. His braced his left arm on the wall above my shoulder, his right snaked around my waist. He dipped his head, his face in my neck. His breath wafted up my neck to my ear. My legs turned weak and the only thing holding me up was his arm.

"Tiffany," his breath said in my ear.

"I hate that name," I groaned.

"Where is Lawrence Marchant?"

So they did not have Lawrence, but *were* after the boy.

His pointed tongue traced the shell of my ear. Heat washed through my body in a delicious wave, coiling inside me, seeping out through my pores, thrilling over my skin. My groin tingled and I gasped aloud.

He stilled, then stepped back, releasing my waist, looking down at the barrel of the Ruger where it dug in his belly. "You would not."

I gasped again, this time in relief, as he eased farther back from me. "I would. I will. Get off my property. You were not invited."

He hissed, lips peeling back to show his teeth. "I am not a vampire. I do not need an invitation."

"Gleaming eyes, pointy teeth; you could have fooled me," I told him sweetly.

He tucked his chin in his neck, frowned, and a look of deep concentration came over his face. Then he changed, right in front of me.

It was slow and it was subtle. Very gradually, his face filled out, eliminating the gauntness. A flush spread over his skin as if the blood came nearer the surface. His teeth blunted and were smooth, dazzling white. His eyes were still a startling blue, but now warm. The metallic luster to his hair faded. And an incredibly handsome, but human man smiled at me as if I were the most wonderful thing he had ever seen.

I gaped. He grinned at my expression. "Interesting. I wonder why convincing *you* I am human takes considerably more effort."

I backed inside, hitting the door hard with my uninjured hip, pushing it open.

He tried to follow me inside but stopped on the doorstep, his right foot an inch from the scattered metal filings. He looked down and hissed again.

I slammed the door.

I went in the kitchen swiping beads of sweat off my face with my sleeve.

Mel and Jack followed me from hall to kitchen. "What are we going to do?" Jack cried.

"We?" Mel asked as she shot to the window and looked out.

Jack stood in front of me and puffed out his chest. "You know I would've seen him off if I could, Tiff."

Mel's laughter pealed through the room. "She knows you're a wuss."

He turned on her. "And you're a lecherous hussy. Gorge this and Gorge that, and how he's such a pretty-boy. You have no idea—"

"Hussy!" Mel shrieked.

"Hussy?" I echoed. Hadn't heard the word used in a long time. I flung up my hands to shoulder level, palms out. "Enough, you guys!"

Mel came over. "We worry about you."

"We would go out of our minds if anything happened to you," Jack said.

A small warmth grew in the region of my heart, but Jack spoiled it by adding, "We'd be back to how it was before you moved in. Me and *her*, standing around doing nothing day in, day out." He stood tall in a dramatic pose. "I think I would kill myself."

Afternoon, and I was *damned* if I would cower in the house all day. I went out to talk to Lindy, toting the Ruger. She looked up in alarm when she saw it.

"Relax, Lindy. It can't hurt you."

She sighed. "I suppose nothing can hurt me now, except the pain in my heart."

She didn't mean it literally; she thought of Lawrence.

I had to tell her he was still missing, but I didn't say anything about his stuff disappearing from the apartment, or nobody remembering him.

She put her hands to her face. "How can he just disappear? Where is he?"

"Perhaps you'd know better than me. Who are his special friends, Lindy? Who would he go to?"

"I don't know who he plays with at school and he's never had a play-date. My poor little boy!"

I couldn't even give her a consoling pat. "Lindy, we will find him. Don't doubt it."

She stumbled to her feet. "I'm going back to the apartment. If he can, he'll go home."

I stood up with her. "It's not your apartment anymore. They've probably already cleared out your stuff." Which, if she did go, could account for Lawrence's things no longer being there.

"Lawrence won't know."

"You tried it before and you couldn't leave the yard."

But she tried again, picking up speed as she moved away from the fruit trees. She stopped suddenly as if she hit an invisible wall. She stood still a moment, then tried again. Same result. She sagged, shoulders slumping.

Something she said sent my mind spinning, something I completely blew off before. "... *except the pain in my heart.*"

Her heart. She had a blurred memory of a tall, yellow-haired figure *coming right at her.* She didn't see him properly, but that didn't matter because unless their killer is behind them, the dead see with something other than their eyes. *I* need a clear visual, but the dead don't. *She didn't remember his face.*

The demon did not kill her. She *did* die a natural death.

She should not be here.

But he touched her at the moment of death. He enabled her spirit to wander. And she came to me. If she hadn't, no one would know about Lawrence.

The demon did not kill her. Did he send her to me?

The phone rang. I hurried inside and saw Mike's number on Caller ID. I grabbed the phone. "Hi, Mike," I said a little breathlessly.

"Can you come down here?" he asked.

I glanced back to make sure Jack and Mel were elsewhere. "What do you need?"

He sounded irritable. "To talk to you. Here. In my office."

"Righty-ho. You gonna give me an idea why?"

"No."

I didn't particularly want to chat with Mike when he was in this mood. "How about I'm there in. . . ." I glanced at the big pink-framed wall clock. "An hour?"

"Now."

I narrowed my eyes. Mike's terse one-liners made me less than cooperative. "Sorry. I'm busy. I'll see you in an hour."

"It's about Lawrence Marchant," he said.

I stopped just inside the Squad Room to look at the wall, where Royal Mortensen's picture hung with the rest of the gang's. I silently whistled.

What a *hunk!* An exotic-looking man with a lean, chiseled face, straight nose and full lips, blond highlights in his long glossy-brown hair, skin nicely bronzed. His deep-brown, tip-tilted eyes caught the light, sparkling with good humor. A white T-shirt clung to broad shoulders and a narrow waist, an impressive chest with sculpted abs and nicely rounded pecs. I grinned at the picture—Clarion PD had itself a poster boy.

I didn't see him as I headed for Mike's office. I would have noticed. Penney and Garn nodded. Brad Spacer saluted me with his oversize coffee cup.

I tapped on the doorframe. "Mike?"

At his desk, Mike beckoned me. "Take a seat, Tiff."

I faced him across his paper-strewn desk. He cleared his throat a couple of times before he spoke. Not a good sign. "Uh, Tiff?"

"Yes, Michael."

"Lawrence Marchant. Birth certificate, school records, medical and dental history. . . ."

I could have said something scathing, but I was too worried.

"We talked to the neighbors again. They swear they don't recall any child living with Lindy Marchant." He scratched his head behind his ear. "Three of them agreed to a polygraph. They're telling the truth, or think they are. It doesn't make sense." He eyed me like he hoped I could solve the mystery.

"I have no idea what's going on, Mike. Only know what I got from his mother."

He continued to stare at me, as if trying to gauge my reaction, and I got edgy. I couldn't tell him what I knew, so I tried to look baffled. I knew more was coming as Mike would not have called me to his office if he had good news. So I said nothing as I watched a deep frown etch his forehead.

But neither did he. He was the first to look away.

"What gives, Mike? What do you know about Lawrence?"

"This is bigger than the disappearance of one child. I spoke to Agent Larsen earlier."

The FBI? What now?

He looked in my eyes again. "You know how many kids go missing each year, here in the States? We're talking hundreds of thousands under eighteen-years-old. So I'm not surprised it took this long to make the connection."

My breath caught in my throat. "Connection?"

"More than two hundred of those kids were born on November 9, 2002. Same as Lawrence Marchant." Mike looked away; he couldn't meet my eyes now. "And we just started looking. There could be more, a lot more."

He ran his palm down his face, but that didn't erase the rigid lines on his forehead and beside his mouth. "Some bright spark at the Bureau saw a communication from Interpol and joined the dots. Same thing's been happening all over the world."

"The world?" I repeated inanely. I couldn't quite coordinate my thoughts.

"Lawrence Marchant's disappearance is part of a pattern. Male children born on November 9, 2002, have been disappearing *since* then."

I tried to speak and stuttered the words instead. "*Since* 2002? But, you mean babies, toddlers. . . ."

His voice softened. "I know."

A dead silence hung between us for a few seconds.

"I know missing children aren't your field, but I'd like you with us on this. You put us onto Lawrence and I think you have an interest in finding him."

I cleared the lump in my throat. "Believe me, I do have an interest in tracking down Lawrence, and even if I'd never heard of the boy, do you think I'd say no to finding a missing child? But why do you think I'd be of any help, Mike?"

"You said you. . . . You said. . . ." He cleared his throat and tried again. "You communicated with his mother. Maybe she knows something," he said uncomfortably.

Lindy didn't appear to know anything helpful, but I didn't tell Mike. "I'll do my best."

"Good. I thought you'd agree. I want you and Roy working together on this."

What? I was not a cop and had never been asked to partner with one. Surely Mike could see the difficulties posed by such a partnership? He thought I *contacted* the dead, he didn't know I saw and heard them. Cops are method, logic and evidence while I'm anything but. I could see Mortensen asking me for the names of my *sources* and insisting I rigidly follow police procedure, and not believing a single word I said anyway.

With a thin smile, I said, "Um, no."

His smile was just as narrow. "I thought you'd say that, but I want you to reconsider. If you don't work with Roy, you're out. I'll get a C & D from Judge Michaels."

I gripped the wood arms of the chair. "You'll put a Cease and Desist on me? You're kidding, right?"

He slowly shook his head side to side. "Lawrence Marchant is our business now. If you won't work with us, you'll get in our way."

I gave him a murderous look. "I'm a private citizen, Mike. You can't stop me."

"Yes, I can."

And he could, too. Damn the man.

"And if you work for me, you get paid," he added.

I leaned back in the chair and folded my arms over my chest, compressing my lips stubbornly. "You know what people think of me, I'm a whacko. Mortensen won't listen to anything I tell him."

Mike's shoulders relaxed. "Give him a chance. He wasn't surprised when I told him what you do. He worked with a psychic on a couple of cases in Seattle. Told me the experience totally rearranged his thinking on metaphysical investigation."

Metaphysical investigation? They have a name for it now?

"Tiff?"

I waved at him. "Give me a minute." The upside, I would be in on anything the cops learned about Lawrence. The downside, I would be stuck with Royal Mortensen breathing down my neck. But he could go where I couldn't without a damned good reason. He could open doors.

"Okay," I agreed. "But you tell Mortensen we're partners. He's not my boss."

"Already done, Tiff. Already done," he said smugly.

I started to my feet, but Mike saved the whammy for last. "One more thing. Some of the children were found. They were murdered."

And while I was still trying to absorb that, he looked past me at the big plate-glass window separating his office from the squad room. "Roy's here. Come meet him."

I followed Mike inside the Squad Room and to a side office. He called through the door, "Roy, Tiff's here."

Detective Royal Mortensen came out of the office. I took a step back, almost tripping over my feet as what I saw registered. Mike said something to Mortensen and looked back at me. He put his hand on the guy's shoulder. "Tiff, meet Roy Mortensen."

To Mortensen he said, "Roy, meet Tiff Banks and if you know what's good for you, don't call her Tiffany. She's partnering with you on the Marchant case."

Royal Mortensen presented his hand. I stared, and I cannot even begin to picture my expression. Dumfounded. Horrified. Incredulous. Take your pick. His hand dropped and the half-smile slid off his face.

Six-foot-six? Shining metallic copper hair threaded with strands of gold, clipped back in a pony tail. His tip-tilted eyes sparked and glowed a deep brown like newly minted pennies. Wide shoulders strained a black tee tucked in khaki pants with his ID badge pinned to the waistband.

He was so much more than his picture.

I looked at Mike, then back to Mortensen, wondering what Mike saw when he looked at him. *I do not believe this!*

Those little cogs and gears in my head clicked and dropped into place. The process normally felt good, but not this time. Kids born six years ago, disappearing over the past six years. Mortensen had been a detective for the past six years.

Demons were involved.

Mortensen was a demon.

"Forget it," I growled, and stalked away.

I stepped outside to a cool Clarion evening, the sun descending in the west and flaming distant peaks with crimson. Down the street, the neon on the new Megaplex center flashed a bright, green welcome. People entered the impressive portal of the Clarion Hilton across the street in ones and twos, from their attire going to some fancy function. The Golden Spike Bank advertised a drop in home mortgage interest rates with a huge banner slashed across its face.

What am I going to do? A demon in the Clarion PD. And he was ideally placed to *make* those little boys disappear. With Mortensen on Lawrence's case, the kid would never be found. He'd make sure of that.

Who to talk to? Only Lynn, and she couldn't help me. I was on my own.

"Miss Banks!"

Mortensen trotted down the steps before I could get in my car. I stood with my back to him, frozen in place. My heart pounded as if trying to jackhammer out my chest.

"I think I—" he began.

"I know what you are," I blurted as I turned to face him.

He looked amused. "I'm sure Mike gave you the rundown, and—"

"I *know* what you are!" I growled. "I'm psychic. I see you as you really are."

He tucked his chin in his neck, his expression wry. "And what am I,

Miss Banks?"

"I don't know what you call yourself, Mister Pointy Teeth. You tell me."

I got in my car and drove off, leaving him on the curb, looking after me. He wasn't smiling anymore.

Chapter Eight

— ♈ —

I like a hearty breakfast, but not taking the time to prepare one. Toasted frozen waffles are not bad when you slather them with strawberry preserve and a squirt of the stuff supermarkets call whipped cream. Mel and Jack watched me swallow every mouthful.

They don't remember the taste of food, but watching me eat fascinates them. Sometimes they ask me to describe flavors, but since they have no point of reference, what I say makes no sense to them. They still ask.

As their eyes tracked each forkful of waffle, I wondered they were not bored. I was totally their world, their drama and their amusement. Yes, shades still experience the entire spectrum of emotions, including envy.

"What *are* you going to do about him?" from Jack.

"Obviously she can't do anything," Mel said.

"There has to be *something* I can do," I replied fretfully, "but I can't think of a thing."

I chewed slowly, strawberry and cream and a slightly rubbery pastry-like product. I would have liked to believe Mortensen was a *nice* demon, if there were such a thing, but what I knew of them pointed to the opposite.

Mortensen was in solid with the cops, too.

I couldn't work with him. And after opening my big mouth, I could have three demons coming after me instead of two. What made me let on I knew about him? *What happened to common sense, Tiff? Where did you lose that edge you're so proud of?*

Did Mortensen hex me so I couldn't think straight? My hand twitched, making my fork chime on the rim of the plate. But I didn't feel anything from Mortensen, nothing like the power of the black-haired demon as he pinned me to the ground.

I didn't care what Mike said or what he laid on me, official or otherwise. I would find Lawrence Marchant, and I'd do it alone. I would start at Mary Frances, talk to Lawrence's teacher. A mother does not always perceive her children as others do; other people could give me a different picture of Lawrence. And, talking of pictures, I would like one of the boy.

"Visitor!" Mel chimed the same time as the doorbell.

Would I ever again have a peaceful, uninterrupted morning?

"Tiff," Jack hissed. "It's one of *them*."

Please, be mistaken, I anguished. I pushed my plate away, got up, crept to the hall and stuck my head around the kitchen doorframe far enough I could see through the glass either side of the front door. A frisson of foreboding shuddered down my back. Royal Mortensen stood on my doorstep.

He looked luscious in a black, silky short-sleeved shirt tucked in tight black jeans, his badge clipped to his front left pocket. Any other man I would have called crazy for wearing a thin shirt in November, but maybe demons didn't feel the cold. He wore a shoulder holster. I wondered what gun he used, so he could safely handle the metal.

He didn't look any less beautiful for looking more like a human than a demon. But his hair was still metallic copper and gold, and his eyes an incredible burnished brown.

"Now he is what I call drop-dead gorgeous," Mel said.

"Har har," from Jack.

The bell chimed again.

"Don't let him see you! Pretend you're out," Jack hissed in my ear.

I leaned away from him. Touching Jack hurts neither of us, but it would be an intrusion, so we try to respect each other's space. "My car's out there," I whispered.

"Miss Banks? I know you're home. Please open the door."

"He doesn't know. He can't," Mel said.

Mortensen slid his hands in his hip pockets and looked through the glass. I ducked back in the kitchen. "I heard you on the phone," he called out.

"The phone?" from Jack.

"He must have heard me talking to you guys, but knows I'm alone."

"*Thinks* you're alone," Mel corrected.

I peeked through the hall again. Mortensen propped his hip on the glass. "We can work together, Tiff. We can find Lawrence Marchant. Just give me a chance." He peered through the glass again. "I'm not going anywhere until we talk."

Oh hell. I recognized the stubborn set of his jaw for what it was. He would wait all day. "I'm going out," I said told Jack and Mel. "Don't sidetrack me."

I pulled up to my full height, ran my palms down my hips to wipe the sweat off them, and with a single deep breath, went in the hall and to the door. *You'll be fine,* I told myself. I just had to remember what he really was.

I opened the door and glowered at him.

Mortensen smiled slightly. "Miss Banks. May I come in?" And he stepped right over the steel filings still scattered on the floor.

I backed up, speechless, every profanity I knew on the tip of my tongue, too astonished to spew them out.

He walked past me, along the hallway like he owned the place and in the kitchen. "May I?" he asked, pulling out a chair and sitting at the table.

I followed him in. "No, you may not. Get out."

"But I just got here. Mm, waffles." He looked over at the toaster. "Any to share?"

I was frustrated and afraid. A demon in my home! "You leave my house right now!" I spluttered.

Jack and Mel shrank in the corner of the room near the backdoor.

I unclipped my charm bracelet and threw it at him. He caught it in one hand. "Pretty, in a metallic kind of way."

Mouth open, I sank to the chair opposite him. "How can you—"

"No. How can you?" He dropped the bracelet on the table top with a little clatter. "I've worked with mediums and psychics before—how can *you* know what I am?"

So much for the *let me in so we can help Lawrence Marchant* routine. I crossed my arms on my chest and hunched my shoulders. "I'm not sitting here in my own house, in my own kitchen, answering your questions."

He reached behind his neck with both hands to adjust the strip of leather which bound back his glorious hair, and my gaze was drawn to the muscles of his arms and the way his chest expanded. I had to concentrate on his words when he said, "Then why don't we trade information? You answer my question, I answer yours."

"Do it," Jack said.

"Why?"

"It seems fair." Mortensen told me.

"Because you could *learn* something," from Jack.

Like what? As if Mortensen would be honest. I couldn't believe anything he told me. And I definitely did not want to share what I knew with him.

There again, being a demon himself, Mortensen must know his buddy demons chased me, and why. He'd know whether one of them did something to Lindy. He knew more than me. Maybe he would slip up.

I realized I was locked into his incredible brown eyes, and blinked. I also realized my fascination, not any arcane demon powers, pulled me in. I gave my head a quick little shake to shake me out of it. "I don't want to know anything about you."

"But you already know quite a lot about me and my people if I'm not mistaken," he said smoothly. "Yet you told no one. You are a rarity, Miss Banks."

"No, but I'm not an idiot either. Who would believe me?"

"True," he said with a nod. His fingers stroked the poorly applied white paint of the tabletop; long, lean fingers moving in a caress, as if he touched skin, not wood. "So, what have we? We have already established I am not of any race native to your world. What else do you want to know?"

I couldn't ignore the opportunity. "Where do you people come from?" I asked.

"Could be difficult to explain."

I rolled my eyes to the ceiling. "I knew it!"

"We did not come from another world," he went on. "We live here, on Earth, as you do but in a different . . . sphere, or dimension. You could say we occupy a different space."

"Sure," I said with perfect understanding. Not! "You watch too many sci-fi movies."

He put his head back and laughed, a warm, rich baritone which made my skin tingle in a far from unpleasant way. He met my gaze, amusement making his eyes shine, and slid the bracelet across the table to me. "Here."

I took it and refastened it on my wrist. "How come alloy doesn't bother you?"

He traced a pattern on the table top with one finger. I wished he would look someplace else, because his deliberate concentration on my face discomfited me. "We become inured to it if we remain here for a long time. Those of us who were born here, like me, have no problem with alloys."

That widened my eyes. "You were born here?"

"Many of us form relationships with your people, have children, careers, spend our lives here. From you we get a certain, well, pleasure we don't experience with our own kind."

I grimaced. "You're talking about sex."

His expression was serious. "Yes and no." Then he widened his eyes theatrically. "What, do you think our own women are lacking in that department? But you give us something above and beyond sex. It is . . . pervasive."

"You feed off us."

A chuckle burst out of him. "Where did you get that idea? It just feels damned good, Tiff!"

And they also used what *feels damned good* to control us, like the other two demons tried with me.

Something he'd said posed a question. If they formed relationships with human beings, and had children . . . . "You have babies, the same way we do. I mean how our women do?" I felt my face redden at how stupid that sounded coming out my mouth.

He rolled his eyes. "No, we lay eggs and hatch them—of course we have babies! We think the reason we can enter your reality so easily is we are very like you."

"How, like us?"

He leaned in. His gaze bore into me. "Physically."

I almost gulped aloud. Avoiding his eyes, I laid my arms on the table and twined my fingers together, concentrating on my nails. "How many of you are here?"

"Here? You mean worldwide? Many of us; although we gravitate to the highly populated areas. My turn. Why can you see my true form?"

I shrugged a shoulder. "I don't know. I see supernatural beings. That's all there is to it. Don't know why. Don't know how."

I sounded calm, but a part of me was somewhere else, looking down at the stupid woman having a casual conversation with a demon. "How long have your people been here?"

He smiled and looked down at his moving finger, still making invisible patterns on the table. Tiny laugh lines formed at the corners of his mouth. "We have been here for a very, very long time, Tiff." He looked up, laying his palm flat on the table.

With an inward shiver, I reminded myself I faced a dangerous man. I needed the reminder, because as we talked I was letting my guard down, feeling comfortable sitting at my table with a supernatural . . . something, and I was defenseless. My gaze flicked to the kitchen drawer where I kept the Ruger.

I leaned back in my chair. "Your turn, Roy."

"I prefer Royal."

Did I really just call him Roy! I was losing it, and fast. What was wrong with me? Was he working his magic on me after all? Surely I would know if he were.

"And I'd prefer you call me Miss Banks," I snapped.

He raised his arms, holding up his hands placatingly, and for a second, musculature bulging all over the place hypnotized me. "A change of attitude would benefit both of us."

"You mean a change in my attitude."

"You have to trust me."

I planted my palms on the table top and half rose to my feet. "Trust you?" *When your friends attacked me? When they came to my house, asking me where Lawrence is? When you just happened to be where boys like Lawrence disappeared in the past six years?*

Disappeared, and died. Mike didn't tell me how many were murdered. He knew it would be more information than I wanted.

Okay, the conversation was over. If anyone let something slip, it would be me. "You get one more question, then you leave."

"I had but one and you answered it, if in an unsatisfactory way."

I got to my feet. "Then this is good-bye, Detective."

He looked up at me quizzically. "You don't want to know more?"

I had a ton of questions, but this felt too much like consorting with the enemy. I mutely shook my head as I glared at him. I could no longer trust my own mouth.

He rose to his feet and left the house.

"That went well," Jack said.

"Hm. What?" Mel said.

Jack shook his head. "Did you get any of that, or were you too busy slobbering over him?"

Here we go again, I thought as they squared off.

Colin and I went to a movie followed by dinner at Arrivederci, our favorite Italian restaurant and no relation to the chain in Arizona. As always, the tiny eatery was packed and loud with the clink of utensils and chink of glassware, the chefs and waiters yelling at one another in Italian, and Frank

Sinatra crooning in the background. It was not conducive to conversation and I was glad, because I didn't feel like talking. I did eat, but mostly I fiddled with my fork and Colin kept reminding me my dinner was getting cold.

Every now and then he looked at me with concern and I thought to myself, *what a nice guy*. And right then I realized two things. I had already decided I would eventually lose Colin, just as I lost other boyfriends. And Jack and Mel were not to blame for my doomed relationships. I was to blame.

I lied to them, about everything, and a relationship based on lies cannot survive. I was too worried about what they would think of me to tell them the truth. I thought the truth would drive them away, but *I* drove them away. I didn't even have the guts to tell Colin what I did for a living.

"Col," I said, "what do you think of the supernatural?"

He tucked his chin in his neck and a lock of fine blond hair fell over his forehead. "Supernatural? What do you mean?"

I made a face. "You know . . . ghosts."

He grinned. "It's rubbish, isn't it."

"Is it? A lot of people have seen ghosts. They can't all be wrong."

He dabbed at his mouth with his napkin, folded it and put it neatly by his empty plate. "People see what they want to see, Tiff. We love mystery and myth. We keep the tales going through the centuries." He threaded his fingers together and folded his hands on the tablecloth. "People who *think* they see ghosts are deluding themselves."

Oh.

I leaned back in my chair with one arm hooked over the back. "So you won't even entertain the possibility?"

He suddenly chuckled. "Don't tell me you thought you saw a ghost!"

"Of course not," I said with a small smile.

He reached over the table and took my hand. "I'm a down-to-earth kind of guy. I've never understood the need some people have to believe in all that otherworldy crap."

Otherworldy. So of course I spent the rest of the evening thinking of Royal

Mortensen.

I didn't go to Colin's apartment after supper. I told him I was too tired, and I told myself I didn't want him to see the road rash down my leg. I lied about the wrist, saying I sprained it when digging weeds. I went home to my prying roommates.

Chapter Nine

Mike wanted me to work with Royal and I needed the money. And I still thought I could learn something from the demon. Not from another question and answer session, because he could tell me anything and I would not know truth from fiction, but I still hoped he'd let something slip.

I learned that like the stereotypical cop, the demon variety favor coffee and donuts for breakfast and can eat with nary a speck of powdered sugar falling on their brown leather jacket.

Demons eat our food. Demons drink coffee. Big deal.

Driving with Royal unsettled me. He was hot, in more ways than one. Warmth seemed to emanate from him and bathe my side from hip to head. His left hand lay on his thigh, and each time I glimpsed it from corner of my eyes, I recalled the black-haired demon's supple fingers.

I turned off the car's heater and fixed my gaze on the road ahead. He tried to speak to me, but gave up and nibbled on another donut after five minutes of me grunting out one-word replies.

But I wanted to talk. I really wanted to ask. Did his kind really come from another world, or whatever, or was it baloney? But why bother to make up such a tale? Why not try to convince me he was just a regular Joe? And what *about* Royal Mortensen—was he married, with little demon brats running around his ankles? How long had he been in Clarion? Where did he live? My eyes slid to him and away. He looked ahead, but he smiled.

An old Catholic school built of big blocks of stone, Mary Frances has the attributes which make a church-run school feel like a church: lofty ceilings, arched doorways, narrow windows more like slots. Our footsteps tapped briskly on the cold flagstone floor as I walked along a cloister-like passageway with Royal a step behind. A nun in full habit wafted down a side passage as we passed it, her steps silent.

Lawrence's teacher, Father Robert, awaited us in his office just off the assembly hall. Bookshelves and big old pieces of furniture crowded the room and stacks of paper lay everywhere: on his desk, the three chairs, two high tables and on the edges of the bookshelves, pushed up against the books. He cleared some off the two chairs facing his desk, looked about for somewhere to put them and ended up stacking them on the floor below the big bay window. Royal's arm brushed mine as I lowered myself to one of the chairs and I felt a tiny thrill of sensation.

After a polite welcome, Father Robert steepled his fingers and gazed solemnly at us over them. "I was very sorry to hear about Lawrence's mother; we all were. Totally unexpected. She was so young."

I expected him to say it was God's will Lindy died, but he didn't. I was glad, because that statement always raises my hackles.

"Did Lawrence have any visitors? Did you see him with another adult besides his mother?" Royal asked.

"We allow visitors only with the permission of the parent, and it is generally related to the student's education or Saint Mary Frances activities."

"Did Lawrence have any as such?"

Father Robert shook his head. "Not that I know of."

"You do know Lawrence is missing?"

"So we were informed. We wondered if Lawrence saw his mother die and ran away."

I wondered the same thing. I wondered if the boy saw his mother's murderer.

"We'd like to talk to his friends, with their parents' permission of course. Could you give us names and addresses?"

Father Robert's gaze slipped past us, over our heads, as if studying the wainscoting. "I don't know how to respond, Detective. Lawrence does not really have friends, not in the sense he has playmates." His eyes half closed. "I would have to describe them more as . . . fans? Followers?"

I glanced at Royal, but he stared at Father Robert. "I don't get you, Father," I said.

"Lawrence's relationship with the other pupils at Saint Mary Frances is . . . unusual, in that he does not foster friendship with them, but they are nonetheless attracted to him. I have watched them at recess. They gather around him. I don't think he understands it himself. He appears bemused by their attention."

"Surely he's just a popular child with his own little clique?"

Father Robert smiled. "Believe me, I am not normally one to wax lyrical. Lawrence is a quiet, well-behaved, studious child, yet I feel he holds himself apart from everyone but his mother. Not as if he is better than anyone else, rather he is . . . removed from the mundane world."

That was *deep* and I didn't know what to make of it.

"Then we would like names and addresses of his classmates, if it is no bother," Royal said as if Father Robert had not just said something which sounded decidedly creepy.

"Of course not." Father Robert took a ledger from a desk drawer and started to copy names and addresses on a sheet of foolscap.

"Do you have a photo?" I asked.

He looked up, then groped through a pile of papers on his desk. "Lieutenant Warren said you would need one. Ah, here it is."

Royal and I looked at the photo. A standard school photo, but Lawrence was anything but standard. He was a beautiful child with long, shoulder-length, glossy brown hair and bright blue eyes, his face the same pointed shape as his mother's. He didn't smile in the photo, but his eyes seemed to glimmer. It must have been a trick of the light.

***

I drove, since Royal didn't have his own car. He claimed he had not found the time to shop for one. He could have taken one from the pool, but at least I would get mileage reimbursement.

Money was a major issue for me. Laid off from Bermans, the telemarketing company I worked at for four years, I should have been out job hunting, but I hadn't had the time since Lindy turned up. With a fraction over five hundred dollars in savings and my checking account an embarrassment, I was thankful I owned my house, but the annual property taxes were due and up another hundred since last year. I needed to renegotiate my fee with Clarion PD.

Royal flipped through Lindy's file again. "An only child. Mother and father deceased. Her only living relative is an aunt in Chicago, who's in her eighties." He looked over at me. "The woman was all alone in the world. Do you know who fathered Lawrence?"

The question surprised me. And what an odd way to phrase it: *fathered*. I took my eyes off the road a moment to glance over at him. "Is it important?"

"If Lawrence knows who his father is, he could be trying to reach him. Or, if he's local, already be with him."

"Hm. I never thought of that." I stared at the road ahead. "But I'm not a detective."

I had a little difficulty with my driving if I didn't concentrate. Royal's presence filled my little Forrester. I felt a wash of heat tingling down my right side. Actually, it was downright pleasant, but also extremely distracting. I thought he knew the effect he had on me because every now and then he smirked.

My thoughts wandered, and I was having a nice little daydream I would rather keep to myself when Royal's hand on my shoulder shocked me right out of it. "Tiffany?"

"Don't call me that!"

He grinned at me as he pointed through the windshield. "I thought that would get your attention. You almost went in the back of that pickup."

I eased off on the gas. "Get in the back."

"What?"

"If you want to be a back-seat driver, assume the position."

He chuckled. Did all demons have such a cute chuckle?

I indicated right and checked my rear-view mirror, and almost choked.

Two demons in the black SUV behind me. They were right up my rear end so I got a good look at them. I was pretty sure one was Caesar and the other had long black-red hair.

I grit my teeth and swung the Subaru to the right lane. Royal grabbed the arm rest. "Tiff?"

The SUV swerved in behind me. "Shit!"

Royal eyed a question at me, but I couldn't speak. Stuck with a demon in my car and two others following me—*what the hell do I do now?*

Royal saw me glance in the rearview mirror. He twisted to look behind us.

We roared down Wendover Avenue and the demons—I should say the *other* demons—came right behind us. I cranked the wheel to the right and took us onto Adams. I admit I felt panicked, torn between screeching to a stop and jumping out of the car, or driving as recklessly as I could without hitting something, hoping I could lose them and keep Royal off balance.

I risked another glance in the mirror. The demons were dropping back.

Royal yelled "Stop!" right in my ear.

I don't know if surprise made me do it, but I did just that. I reflexively stamped my foot on the brake and the Subaru, like the obedient little girl she was, instantly obeyed, sending us into our seat belts. But Royal was out the car in a flash.

Appalled, I watched him charge the car behind us. He didn't pull his gun, he just charged. Another surprise: instead of acting like I'd been served to them on a platter, the demons tried to back up. They looked as frantic as I felt. The passenger yelled at Caesar and both alternately looked behind them and back at their buddy demon, who was almost on the hood of their car.

I reached across the passenger seat, pulled the door shut, and put my foot down. I roared away in a cloud of dust and burning rubber.

Chapter Ten

"You have to talk to someone," Mel said.

"Like, who?"

"Mike Warren knows you well enough to believe you. Doesn't he?"

I let my head fall in my hands. "I get results. When Clarion PD loans me out to another department and I get results, they get kudos. He thinks I'm a psychic and he's almost comfortable with what I do, to the point he sees it as a useful specialty. He is *not* going to believe a crazy story involving demons, and Clarion PD's new blue-eyed boy is one." I looked up at her. "And what happens when Mike tells Mortensen what I say? Because it's exactly what he'll do, and Mortensen won't like that, not one little bit."

"But you think Mortensen knows what really happened to Lindy," Jack pointed out. "And his cohorts are after you."

I groaned. "I think he does. He *has* to."

"Then you have nothing to lose."

My shoulder twitched. "Easy for you to say, Mister Insubstantial. Ain't a weapon known to man can hurt you."

Mel stood across from me at the kitchen table. "So you wait until he comes for you? He already waltzed right in once. What's stopping him coming back?"

I jumped up and stormed across the kitchen to the cabinets. I got my gun from drawer and took off the safety. "Demon or no demon, this should put a hole in him."

Mel flung her hands up. "You can't, Tiff. It would be murder."

"He's a demon!"

"You're the only person who knows," Jack said. "He's a detective for Clarion PD; they'd throw away the key."

Right. My stomach churned queasily as I sank back in my chair, clutching the Ruger.

Mel came up to me and put out her hand as if to touch my shoulder, then her hand fell to her side. "You could run away."

"Temporarily," Jack added hastily.

"Just until it's safe and you could come home," Mel said.

I mulled it over. Could I get away? Could I go far enough, the demons couldn't follow?

Could I leave Lawrence to them, if he was still alive?

I slowly shook my head as I chewed on my lower lip.

"As if I could leave you guys all alone," I said, but I couldn't raise a smile.

I fell asleep after a couple of hours of tossing and sweating. The last time I looked at the clock, it read two in the morning. When I woke, it was four o'clock.

As well as the noise from the old heating system, my house likes to creak and groan as it settles down for the night. I know its noises, so I knew the creak in my bedroom did not belong. Someone was in here with me.

I slowly groped for the Ruger, fingers inching under the spare pillow, feeling for metal. I left my hand there and rolled on my back.

I made a few muffled noises and rolled to the side of the bed farthest from the door, sliding the Ruger under the edge of the duvet, pretending I moved in my sleep. I know every inch of my bedroom and presumably the intruder did not, and unless he possessed uncanny night vision, I held the advantage. If I could get on the floor. . . .

The overhead light came on, blinding me. I sat up blinking, the gun in both hands panning around the room as my senses strained. A few unlikely scenarios spun through my head: An unarmed crook? Colin sneaking in to surprise me? I couldn't shoot randomly.

But no, Royal leaned on the doorframe with one hand on the light switch, very natty in a short-sleeved, pale-gold shirt, black slacks and black leather loafers. I pointed the gun at him, pleased my hands barely shook.

"How do you know those men?" he asked.

I was way past the talking stage. I licked my lips and concentrated on his body language. If he even thought about moving, I *would* shoot him. I steadied my aim.

"You're not going to shoot me."

The air blurred and the gun left my hand. He sat on the side of my bed. Confused, astonished, I tried to scoot back and his hand clamped on my thigh right where it hurt. I flinched. He took his hand away as if burned.

He lifted his hands, palm out. "I am not going to hurt you, Tiff. You have my word. But I need answers."

The man had a peculiar affect on me. It seemed my commonsense took a nosedive. I opened my mouth, meaning to tell him to leave and instead it blurted what it should have kept to itself. "One of them was in Coralinda Marchant's apartment when I found Lawrence's drawing."

"What happened?"

"Usual stuff. Chased me, knocked me down, then his buddy tried to take me for a ride." I shrugged. "You know, same old same old."

His fingers wrapped my wrist just below the bandage. "Did they hurt you?"

I looked down. "That? My fault entirely. Silly me. I should know better than jump out a moving vehicle."

His eyes darkened, the pupils stood out like chips of onyx. "They will pay for that."

His chill, implacable tone made me shrink back.

The ice melted from his eyes. He frowned, all concerned-looking. "I frighten you. Do you think I'm like them? Is that it?"

"You're one of them," I growled.

His frown deepened. "Oh. I see."

He had an eyeful of my cleavage and I tried to pull the sheet up higher, but he was sitting on it. The extra pressure put on my various abrasions did not help.

"Now I'm going to tell you what you think," he said.

Oh, yeah? I inwardly sneered. Like I needed another know-it-all guy who thought he had me figured out.

"You think I am in cahoots with the men who chased you."

Well, duh. "They aren't men. You aren't a man!"

"I am, indeed, a man. I am not precisely, physically, built like a human male, but the differences are insignificant."

Not precisely? Whoa! "You didn't seem too surprised to see them."

"I knew they were in Clarion, but likewise, they knew of my presence. This was the first time I got close enough to identify them."

"You knew they were here?" Ditto on the duh. Of course he knew his buddies were in Clarion.

"We sense one another."

Sense? What did he mean? Like Lindy sensed Lawrence? "You did arrest them, didn't you?"

"I let them get away."

I slumped back on the pillows, my mouth curling. "And I'm sure you have a totally logical reason?"

"I will not battle two of my fellows in the middle of town."

"Why not? You're a cop. Cops arrest people all the time."

"They would not have come quietly. It would have been a bloody spectacle. Now I know them, I know where to find them."

I opened my mouth, but he held up one hand. "You believe those men and I are after the same thing, and you are correct."

"Lawrence."

"Lawrence," he agreed. "But I want to help Lawrence. I want to save his life."

"I'm sure their motives are equally pure."

He almost rolled his eyes. Almost. "In my world, as in yours, there are bad guys and there are good guys. I am one of the good guys. I've been trying to get between them and their victims for the past six years. Mostly, I failed."

All those poor little boys.

"As I know who they are now, I can track them. They could lead me to Lawrence. You have to trust me, Tiff."

Trust him? I wanted to and had no idea why. I wanted to believe him. I wanted him to be the good guy. But was it wishful thinking because he was so gorgeous, or did he use demon magic to sway me? Either way, trusting him was not a wise choice, not with what I knew about demons and this one in particular. And he had not said anything to persuade me he told the truth.

All I had was the word of a demon, and sorry, it was not enough.

Another silence with the clock *tocking* in the background and his gaze riveted to my face. I wondered what his hair would look like loose, sliding over his shoulders.

We sat and stared at each other. *Don't look in his eyes, don't look!* I told myself, but I did. He shifted on the bed to face me, leaned in, and I thought he must hear my heartbeat. I forced my body erect, but my nipples embarrassed me by perking beneath my nightgown; loose as it was, they still stood up like happy little miniature mountain peaks. His gaze went to them; he very slowly arched one eyebrow.

I crossed my arms over my breasts. "Cold in here."

Supporting himself with one hand on the mattress, he leaned in yet closer. "It must be you. I feel . . . warm." And the bastard unfastened the top button of his shirt, then the next one down, baring a triangle of smooth pale-copper skin, looking in my eyes all the while.

His eyes twinkled with what could be amusement.

I glared angrily, shamed by my body's response, as I realized he laughed at me. Or . . . teased? He saw my reaction and *teased* me! Teasing was outside my experience. Taunting, yes—kids can be so cruel to one another—teasing, no. The guy had some nerve, waltzing in here and having fun at my expense.

I thought I learned to control my facial expression and body language long ago, but Royal Mortensen read me. What began as a muffled chuckle broke out his mouth as a guffaw. I grew hot with mortification as he composed his features.

He grinned at me as he said in a low, throaty voice, "If I can prove you're wrong in one thing, will you listen to me?"

I hugged myself tighter, said briskly. "Tell me and I'll think about it."

He disarmed me with a broad smile. "I don't have pointy teeth, Tiff."

And he didn't. His teeth were white and even and perfect in his delectable mouth. But that proved nothing, not when I'd already seen a demon alter his entire face. "Huh! Neat trick."

He came in nearer. I tried to disappear in my pillows. "Seriously. I had them capped."

"Capped? So people like me won't know what you are?"

"No." This close, he smelled of sandalwood and amber. "So I can do this." He put his hands on the sides of my face and his mouth fastened on mine.

It was deep and hungry and utterly consuming. His lips were velvet, exploring mine, drawing my breath. I could have *lived* in his kiss for the rest of my life. When he pulled back, a little gasping puff of air escaped my mouth.

And he didn't have pointed teeth.

Stunned. I was stunned by a kiss. *Pervasive?*

His hands still cradled my cheeks, and we gazed in each other's eyes. The only sound was my heavy breathing and the *tock* of the old carriage clock on the mantle. He looked alien, with his parti-colored metallic hair and gleaming eyes, and incongruous against the backdrop of the pastel greens and fawns of my bedroom. His skin was so smooth; it had an ageless quality. And his eyes were depthless.

He let me go and sat back, and I blinked back to the here and now. *He's a demon, Tiff!* I told myself. *Don't let that kiss fool you.*

I licked my lips. "If I ask you to leave, will you?"

"Are you sure you want me to, Tiff?"

"Yes."

He dropped his chin so I couldn't properly see his face.

"Did you really have your teeth capped so you could kiss me?" I couldn't resist asking as he got to his feet.

His smile was slow and wicked. "Well, not you in particular."

And then he was gone.

Damn! Nothing should be able to move so fast!

"If a man kissed me like that I'd be ripping his clothes off, not pissing him off."

My mouth dropped open and I twisted to look at the corner of the room near the window. Mel stood against the wall next the fireplace, Jack beside her.

"What were you two in life? Peeping Toms?"

Jack pushed away from the wall. "Did you hear the one about the dead Peeping Tom?"

"Out! Or God help me I will call in an exorcist!"

They headed for the door, noses in the air. "Wait!" I called as a nasty thought hit me. "A guy saunters in, and you don't warn me?"

Mel put one hand to her hair. "Why would we?"

Puzzled, I rubbed at the headache forming between my brows. "He broke in."

"He didn't," Jack said. "He had a key." He shared a look with Mel. "He did have a key?"

"Seemed so. He came up the path, the deadbolt opened, he came in, threw the bolt, and trotted upstairs."

He has a key to my house! Outrage all but overwhelmed me, and it showed, because my roommates backed to the door. "He had a key," I seethed. "You thought I expected him."

Jack's chin went up and down like a yo-yo.

"You mean you didn't?" Mel asked in a tiny whispering voice.

I threw my hands in the air and fell back on the bed.

***

I went through the house, checking doors and windows. All closed, all secure. He *must* have a key, or lock picks, which would surprise me less than a key. I secured the heavy bolts at top and bottom of the back and front doors. *Nobody* could get those doors open now short of dynamiting them.

If someone really wants in your house, they will find a way, but now Royal would have to break glass to reach those bolts. I'd hear breaking glass.

I got back in bed and snuggled down under my duvet, but in my cool bedroom I felt too hot. Not surprising, the way he got me all riled up. I kicked at the covers, but I had the sheet beneath the duvet tucked in tight. So I had a tantrum.

I got on my knees and hauled the duvet off the bed so it tumbled to the floor in a heap. Then I tried to pull the sheet free. That didn't work, so I got out of bed and tugged one side out, went around the bed and freed the other side. I dropped it on top of the duvet, and stomped on it.

Wisely, Jack and Mel did not reappear in the room.

Tripping on the duvet, I went to the window. I rested my elbows on the sill, clasped my hands and put my mouth on my knuckles. It was early morning now, and the frosty grass in the backyard glittered in the light of a crescent moon. The fruit trees were almost bare. Poor naked Lindy sat beneath the apple tree, arms holding her bend knees, impervious to the cold but not to her grief.

Lawrence. That was the important thing. Find Lawrence and give his mother the peace she deserved. Forget hair which looked like metallic silk and warm copper-penny eyes. Forget a taut body and manipulative lips. He was a demon. I couldn't trust him.

With a moan, I dug my fingers in my hair. Unfortunately, where Royal Mortensen was concerned, I couldn't, apparently, trust myself.

Chapter Eleven

—♈—

I woke to the smell of frying bacon. And was that sausage?

Hot, sweaty, my braid coming apart, I looked for my Ruger and found it on the bedside table where Royal left it. Not bothering with my robe, I crept from the room and stood at the top of the staircase.

Funny. Where were Jack and Mel? They should be in my bedroom, in a panic, shouting in their whispering voices for me to wake.

I inched down the stairs, cautiously stepping over the one which creaks, gun at the ready. Don't tell me a burglar will not cook breakfast; you read about it happening all the time. Intruders don't just break in and steal your stuff nowadays, they eat your food, watch your TV and drink your beer.

I crossed the hall, put my back to the wall, and looked around the doorframe to the kitchen.

I do not believe it! Royal stood at the stove with his back to me, busily stirring in my small nonstick pan with a wooden spoon. My big cast iron skillet sizzled on another burner, and my electric skillet, on the counter, vented steam. The oven was on. Jack and Mel stood behind him as close as they could get. Mel had her hands clasped and jiggled on her feet. Jack held his folded hands to his face in an attitude of prayer.

I marched in. "You again! Mortensen!"

Leaving the spoon in the pot, he spun on his heel and his shoulder went through Jack's head. Jack staggered to one side and clutched his cranium. "Ah, he got me. I'm dy . . . ing!"

Mel tittered.

"Mortensen? Royal is easier on the tongue. Try it, Tiff."

"Mortensen, you—"

"I thought after last night—"

"*Nothing* significant happened last night, Detective."

We locked gazes. I gave him my best steely-eyed glare.

A smile twitched the corner of his mouth. "If you say so."

He turned back to the stove and gave the pot another stir. "Please put your pistol down. You don't need it and you are making me nervous."

He didn't appear nervous. He looked relaxed and confident, at home in my kitchen, wearing the same clothes as last night, except his brown corduroy jacket hung from the peg next the backdoor.

Putting the table between us, I carefully laid the Ruger down. Carefully, because I didn't engage the safety. I could snatch it up and fire in a second.

If he didn't take it out my hand again.

I tried reasoning with him. "You have to quit breaking into my house."

He bent over the stove to sniff the pot, the tail of his long copper-gold hair sliding over one shoulder. "Your security measures are pitiful."

"Yeah, well, my alarm system appears to be out," I said, glowering at Jack and Mel.

"I don't recall signing any contract," Jack said.

"You don't have an alarm system," Royal said.

I didn't have a retort. I couldn't say my security measures relied on two dead people, who at the moment were more interested in breakfast than my safety.

"Bacon!" Mel exclaimed. "You never make bacon."

Because I eat at Audrie's Family Restaurant if I want bacon. Audrie's doesn't burn the bacon, or the sausage, and their eggs don't end up the texture of leather.

I sat at the table, fiddling with the end of my braid, trying to think up something scathing to say. But a kind of calm settled over me. Morning sun streamed through the window in the backdoor, the kitchen felt warm and steamy, and the smell of bacon and sausage was *wonderful*. Mel and Jack were either side of Royal like happy, eager kids, chattering about a breakfast they would never sample.

He put his weight on one hip, which drew Mel's attention to how the fabric of his pants hugged his rear end. She looked at his butt, looked at me and sang a refrain: "Do you see what I see?"

Turning to me, Royal pointed at my old refrigerator, which crouches next the backdoor like a giant wad of pink bubblegum. "Do you like milk with breakfast?"

I shook my head. He looked like a smooth-shaven barbarian. Did demons have hair on their bodies? His arms were hairless. I snuck a look at where his shirt gaped open, at a smooth expanse of lightly-bronzed skin with not a hair in sight. If I closed my eyes, I bet I could imagine sleek warmth beneath my palm.

So I didn't close my eyes. I didn't dare.

"You need to air out your living room; it's musty," he surprised me by saying.

What the. . . ? "You snooped through my house?"

He opened the oven door, letting out a blast of heat, and removed a small baking sheet with half a dozen perfectly round, fluffy biscuits. "I spent the night in there."

As I spluttered, beyond words, he quickly whisked the covers off the skillet and electric skillet, loaded a dish and brought it to the table. Still wordless, I gazed at fried potatoes—the real, homemade kind, not those limp, stringy hash-browns—two eggs over-easy, two slices of bacon, and two biscuits covered in creamy sausage gravy.

"Your favorite," he announced.

He must have asked at the precinct; I had breakfast with the guys enough times. "You forgot the melted cheese."

"I will remember next time."

He checked my kitchen clock. "I have to go." Then he dropped a kiss on my forehead and headed for the backdoor, saying, "I'll see you later, sweetheart."

I put my fingers to my forehead. "What the hell! What did you call me?"

Grinning, he grabbed his jacket off the hook and went through door.

"He's very domestic, isn't he," Mel commented.

"He didn't make coffee," Jack provided.

"And he didn't load the dishwasher," from Mel.

I momentarily closed my eyes. "You could have said he spent the night in the living room."

Jack twitched his shoulders. "We didn't know. We only go in there when you do. You know, those twice-a-year excursions to flick dust from one piece of furniture to the next. No wonder it smells like a tomb."

"We had no idea till he sauntered out. He left the house for fifteen minutes or so and came back with a sack of groceries," Mel said. "Then we were . . . distracted."

"Instead of alerting me, you hang over him, drooling over breakfast," I accused.

"The guy let himself in the house as if he had every right to be here!" Jack protested. "Why should we know any different?" He rolled one shoulder. "Anyway, anyone who makes you breakfast can't be all bad."

"Honey, I was drooling over a lot more than breakfast," said Mel. She joined me at the table. "Are you going to eat that, *sweetheart*?"

I smoldered as I drove downtown. How *dare* the man come in my house, spend the night and make breakfast in *my* kitchen! And he thought he was so damned funny with, "I'll see you later, sweetheart." I could see him bouncing back in with, "Honey, I'm home!" or some such nonsense.

Forgetting to be angry, I bit down on a snicker—it was kind of funny. And it was a damn fine breakfast.

He couldn't watch me all the time. I meant to do a little investigating of my own sans Royal Mortensen and I didn't feel at all guilty for ignoring

Mike's directive. Lawrence's disappearance was my case; so what if I accidentally forgot to let my so-called partner know what I was doing?

Armed with a copy of Lawrence's photo, I went to the Swinn's Supermarket nearest Lindy's place, because most of the frozen food in her freezer came from there. I felt really awkward as I went from one employee to another and I expected someone to sic a store manager on me. I flashed my consultant's badge and hoped nobody asked in what capacity I assisted the police department. Nobody asked, nobody called a manager, and nobody recalled seeing Lawrence.

I might have had better luck with Lindy's photo, but the only one available was of her body lying on a mortuary slab. I made a mental note to ask for a copy.

I visited a book-swap store on Charmane Avenue called Books Galore. A couple of books on Lindy's bedside table bore their stamp on the back cover. No luck there either, but the sales assistant suggested I return the next day when the manager came back from vacation.

I hoped Clarion's branch of the Lincoln County Library would get better results. Lindy had a whole stack of books from them. I wondered if anyone from the PD would return them to the library.

They remembered Lawrence. "He comes for Miss Molly's Story Hour every Thursday evening," one of the librarians told me. "I could never forget a face like his. What a little angel. Parents like the story hour because they can safely leave their children with us while they browse the library."

The implications of my questions and flashing the boy's picture in her face sank in. "Oh my goodness! Has something happened to him? Oh! Oh! I remember. His mother died!"

I pushed back a strand of hair escaped from my braid and stuck to the corner of my mouth. "Lawrence is missing. We know very little about Ms. Marchant and we're trying to track down her friends. He could be with one of them. Did she come here with anyone apart from Lawrence?"

She must have been in her seventies, a plump little gnome-like woman who wore face powder much too pale for her, bright-pink lipstick, and dyed her hair the peculiar pale rusty-red some elderly women seem to favor. She put one pudgy hand to her forehead and closed her eyes. "Let me think. Yes." She opened her eyes and squinted at me. "I did see a young man on several occasions. Very tall, with long blond hair and the most beautiful blue eyes."

I perked up. "Do you know his name?"

She put her head on one side and pursed her lips in a cupid's bow, which made her look like a chubby little bird cocking its head. "No. I'm sorry."

"You didn't hear her say it?"

"They were always very quiet when they came, very respectful of library rules."

Which was no help to me at all. But I would turn it over to Mike. Perhaps he could sit the librarian down with a police sketch-artist.

Blond hair. Yellow-haired. There he was again. The man in the apartment the night Lindy died? The way she described the guy's speed, he *must* be a demon. Library guy could be a demon—the librarian would see a regular human male. Was the man in the apartment and the library one and the same? But maybe Lindy had a yellow-haired man friend who accompanied her to the library.

Walking out of the library and down the steps, I paused to slap my forehead with the heel of my hand.

I could always ask her.

Murphy's Law struck again. Lindy was not there.

"Have you seen Lindy today?" I asked Jack.

He went to the window and looked out. "No, but I haven't been looking. Have you misplaced her?"

"Apparently." I went in the pantry and got an empty five-gallon plastic jug off the floor. "Typical! Just when I really need to talk to her."

I put it in the sink and turned on the cold tap. "I guess she managed to take off after all. Wonder if she's at her apartment?"

"And I would know because. . . ?"

"I don't have time to go see. And I don't have time for your sarcasm either, Jackson."

He clapped both hands to his face. "Oh no! It's Monday!"

"Yep." I left the water running to root through the pantry for the supplies I needed.

"Can't you leave him there?"

"Leave who where?" Mel asked as she came in the kitchen.

"Don't be stupid," I told Jack.

"It's Monday," Jack told Mel.

"Oh, good grief; I forgot. What are you doing, Tiff?" she asked.

I came out of the pantry with a small cardboard box containing a loaf of bread and a box of cereal. From the fridge I took sliced lunch meat and a couple of cheese slices. "I have to go to the cabin, and as Janie's place is nearby I'm taking Mac with me. Peace and quiet and a bit of one-on-one will be good for both of us." I put a carton of milk and some plastic sachets of mayonnaise and mustard in the box

"Peace and quiet!" from Jack. "What about us?"

"What about you? I'm sure you'll have a lovely peaceful night."

"I'm sure. But tomorrow morning. . . ."

I tuned them out. They would have to wait. Lawrence Marchant had to wait. Everything had to wait. I was going to get my baby.

MacKlutzy—not to be confused with McClusky—is my seven-year-old black-brindle Scottish terrier and the light of my life. For years, Janie insisted if she just had Mac to herself for a few days she could turn him into a model of doggy good behavior. This was her third attempt. Janie is a professional trainer and Mac is her nemesis.

If his legs were a bit longer, his ears a bit bigger and he were not badly cow-hocked; if he were about three pounds lighter, Mac would be the perfect show animal. Honest. His temperament? A little feisty. Okay, a lot feisty. Royal would not have sauntered into my house if Mac were here. He would have left two seconds after he arrived, maybe with a small ball of fury attached to his calf.

MacKlutzy? He's a klutz. He tends to trip over things when he has his nose to the ground, or leap without looking where he's leaping. No tall, lithe, agile four-footer for me. I much prefer the small, stubby, bumbling type.

Mac has a thing about Jack and Mel. I have no idea if he can actually see them, or just sense them, but he seems to know they're here. He'll go for days ignoring them, then suddenly *charge*. Literally. As my roommates are not physical barriers between Mac and cabinets, chairs and sundry other hard objects, Mac often hits them head on. Luckily, Scottish terriers have very hard skulls, but his unexpected attacks discombobulate Jack and Mel.

"Turn the TV on before you leave," said Jack.

"Sure." I turned on the 19-inch TV on the counter, took the TV listing to the kitchen table and found the page for the evening's television. Mel and Jack looked it over as I made sure I had everything Mac and I needed.

"USA's showing Braveheart," Mel said. "Mel Gibson in a kilt. Blue woad, long unruly hair, muscular thighs. . . ."

"And after it's finished we'll be stuck with solid repeats of The Cosby Show all night," Jack pointed out. "ESPN's got Classis Boxing, Classic Car Auction and American Gladiators."

He just tried to get a rise out of her. Jack doesn't like that kind of show any more than Mel.

"Like hell!" Mel leaned for a closer look at the guide. "HBO. To Die For and Hairspray."

"We don't have HBO," I said. I joined them and looked through the listings. "TNT. Night of the Living Dead."

"Been there, done that," from Jack.

They settled for watching AMC, which gave them an entire night and early morning of Dirty Harry, Magnum Force, and something called Snakes on a Plane. I dreaded to think what would be playing when I got home.

I left them riveted to the television and set off for Janie's place

When MacKlutzy lays his ears back flat on his skull and slits his eyes, he looks positively evil. I have never seen an expression quite like it on another dog. After giving Janie the look, he wrapped his front feet around my arm and clung to me.

"How did it go?"

"He did really well," Janie said. "Look."

She confidently reached out her hand and laid it on MacKlutzy's flat skull. The ears went back, but he didn't lunge or snap.

"Wow!" I was impressed. "You are *good*!"

"That's what reinforcement and half a sack of liver treats gets you."

The supplies were in the front with me, safe from a Mac-attack, and MacKlutzy had a fine time in the back seat with his box of toys, rooting them out and tossing them all over the place. He would be content during the short trip to the cabin.

The cabin was a kind of co-op. When I worked at Bermans and Peter Chasten complained he had to let his little cabin go because the lease skyrocketed, a few of us thought it was a shame. Peter leased the land up in Monchard and built the little cabin. Unfortunately, if he let the lease lapse, he lost the cabin.

Monchard is really close to Clarion, the dirt road leading to it about ten miles up Pineview Canyon, then another three miles in. Once through the gate, you are in undeveloped backcountry. Lessees can erect a small structure in Monchard, but the area doesn't have water or electricity. Anyway, five of us co-opted with Peter and shared the cabin. And it was my turn to go up there and get it tidied up and battened down for the coming winter.

I left the street lights behind as I drove out of Clarion. When I got to the turnoff for Monchard, I flicked on my high beams and crept along. There are moose, elk and deer and they have right-of-way.

Mac got restless. He could smell a hundred and one enticing scents.

"Almost there," I told him as I turned on the narrow trail leading to the cabin.

Light shone through the pines and quaking aspen.

I braked slowly so as not to send Mac flying off the seat, and turned off the engine. Someone was in the cabin.

Chapter Twelve

———♈———

A pickup truck was parked next to the cabin; one of those huge ones with a cab half a mile off the ground and a back seat big enough to sit in comfortably. I couldn't make out the color, but it looked shiny and new.

From the look of it, every oil lamp glowed inside the small log one-story structure.

"Looks like we have visitors, Mac." I reached inside my jacket and pulled out the Ruger, took off the safety, then reholstered it. "You stay here," I told my dog.

The interloper must have heard the Subaru's engine, but nobody came out of the cabin. I slid from car, carefully closed the door behind me and crept along.

Keeping to the trees, I walked abreast of the dirt road. The air was bitterly cold, redolent with pine and rotting forest mulch. I had in mind some hunters took over the cabin. Hunting is permitted if you lease in Monchard, and maybe someone decided to spend the night in relative comfort before they headed farther up the mountain. I could handle one man, but more? The sensible thing to do would be get out of Monchard, drive home and call

Peter.

I circled the cabin and came at it from the side, silently crossing the surrounding thirty-foot swath we kept free of grass and undergrowth. A peaked tin roof tops the small one-room affair of rough-hewn logs, jutting out over small windows. Inside, two bunks, a sofa and armchair, small dinette table and four chairs take up most of the area, with a free space in front of the open fireplace. There are two cabinets, a shelf and a tiny gas stove. No shower, and the toilet, an outhouse, is forty feet away. I hunched beneath a window and eased up just far enough to look inside.

Next minute, I banged open the only door and marched in.

"Coffee?" Royal asked, measuring out tablespoons of ground coffee into the pot. "I just got the fire going, but it should be hot enough to brew. I tried the stove. It does not work."

A few logs smoldered in the fireplace under the iron grid stretched across it, which I sometimes used to slow-cook a stew. I didn't tell Royal the stove was disconnected from the propane; it was the last thing on my mind.

"What. . . ? How. . . ?"

He hoisted an almost empty five-gallon jug and poured water in the pot. "I hope this is not too old. Did you bring more water?"

I felt a headache building. "Mortensen, get out of here."

He took the pot to the fireplace and positioned it on the grid. "Not going to happen, Tiff. Some nasty people are after you, you need protection."

Yes, I needed protection, from him. He came in my house and now the cabin. And I was alone with him, way out in the middle of nowhere. Sure, we were not too far from Clarion, but no one goes to Monchard unless they lease property and I didn't think many, if any, were here at this time of year.

Past experience taught me pulling my gun would be wasted effort. I looked at him, his tight black jeans and a pale-green shirt open at the neck, multicolored hair loose on his shoulders, the lamplight making strands of it glisten. My gaze lingered on his slightly parted lips. Past experience taught me he kissed like no other man alive.

Snap. Out. Of. It!

"How did you know I was coming here? And for that matter, how did you know where *here* is?"

He looked back at me seriously as he crouched at the fireplace. "You won't like it. I have been keeping an eye on you."

So that was it. "You heard me talking about the cabin and got here ahead of me." I imagined him standing outside my house, listening. Hearing voices through walls several feet thick must be a demon thing.

He rose to his feet and went to the cabinet above the shelf. "You surprise me, Tiff. I did not think you were the type to talk to yourself." He got two ceramic mugs and put them on the shelf. He peered in the cabinet. "I don't suppose you brought sugar and creamer?"

I ignored that, and his comment about me talking to myself. "How did you know where to come?"

"We drink it black, then." He frowned. "I'm a detective. Discovering everything there is to know about a person is my job. And a GPS is a wonderful gadget."

I literally felt the outrage creeping through my chest. "You checked me out?"

"You did not do the same with me?"

"No, I didn't." But I wished I had thought of it. "Seriously, you can't stay here. If you won't leave, I will."

He came toward me and I stepped back a pace. He stopped moving. "I'll sleep in the truck. Okay?"

I briskly shook my head. "No, not okay. You've been masquerading as human long enough to know when you've stepped over the line. This is it, Royal. This is the line. I have to work with you, but you have no right intruding in my personal life."

"Did you not hear me say you are in danger?"

I nodded my chin jerkily. "I heard."

"If I can find you, so can they."

I guessed he meant the two demons at Lindy's apartment. "They couldn't, could they, if you'd arrested them."

He sighed audibly and leaned against the counter. "You were right and I was wrong, but apologies do not change a thing. I feel responsible for your safety."

I heard a whine from outside. "Oh, good grief."

Royal straightened up. "What was that?"

I stalked across the room. "My dog. I came here to get the cabin ready for winter. I am going to do that and leave. You can do as you please." I used a hot pad to pick up the coffeepot, and carried it outside. Royal came behind me as I emptied the lukewarm coffee on the ground.

I turned, and he stopped moving. I saw the tension in his body, the stiffness, and realized we were both keeping our distance.

I wanted to reach out and grab him.

He stuck his thumbs in the back pockets of his pants. "I'll wait and follow you back to your house."

I nodded wordlessly, for some inexplicable reason feeling a lump in my throat. I handed him the coffeepot.

Another whine from the car. I stepped down from the porch. "I'm bringing Mac inside."

I drove the car to the cabin and parked out front. I got Mac from the back seat, carried him in the cabin, shoved the door shut with my rear end and put him on the floor.

Royal stood beside the dinette table, body at an angle, supporting himself with one hand. He looked at Mac. Mac looked back.

Mac shot across the floor and his mouth closed on Royal's left ankle.

"Ow!" Royal said. "That hurts."

I smiled admiringly at Mac. "Did you know the jaws of a Scottish terrier can exert two hundred pounds of pressure?"

Royal stood straighter. "About what it feels like."

"His vet says she'd rather be bitten by a German shepherd than a Scottie."

"Is that so?" Royal gave his ankle a tentative wiggle. Mac wiggled right along with it.

I knelt down beside Mac. "Drop it, Mac," I commanded. He rolled his eyes at me and slowly opened his mouth. I took his head in both hands. "Good boy! You must not bite the man, he's. . . ." I was about to say *he's a friend.* I amended that. "You don't know where he's been."

Royal edged back to a chair and sat. He peeled up the leg of his jeans. No socks. "Not a mark."

"He has it down to an art. Mac can bite just hard enough to hurt without breaking the skin."

I headed back to the door. "I'll get his water bowl from the car. Don't let him cock his leg on anything."

"How do I stop him?"

"You yell, *No, bad boy!*"

I went out, closing the door behind me. As I approached the car, I heard, "No! Bad boy!" from the cabin. I smirked.

I got Mac's water bowl and a chew treat and headed back.

The ground in front of me exploded.

I had never been fired at before and I reacted automatically. The ammo bit the dirt in front of me, so I ran in the opposite direction.

I heard Royal yell my name, but another burst of gunfire overpowered his voice.

I charged through the forest, and pretty soon I didn't know where I was or where I was going. I'd walked over much of Monchard before, but in daylight. As I moved farther from the lights in the cabin, I entered the true, deep darkness of night. I could look ahead to avoid trees which loomed up in an instant and trip over an obstacle, or I could look at the ground and slam into a tree. I did both, several times.

I tripped over a fallen branch and fell prone next to a towering aspen. With the wind knocked out of me, I lay there trying to suck air. The silence of the forest closed in on me.

When I could breathe again, I got up on hands and knees. A single bullet hit the trunk of an aspen very near my head and splinters bit into my scalp. I dropped down flat again and crawled forward, using my elbows and toes to propel me along, heading for a clump of undergrowth I could barely see.

You may think you can look after yourself, but being the target of a gun-wielding assassin alters your perspective. Terror tends to numb your brain.

Although it weighed heavy against my ribs, I forgot I carried a weapon until another bullet shattered a small rock next my hand. Then I wondered if shooting at the darkness would pinpoint me. Then I thought, *stupid, they already know where you are.* I rolled on my back, sat up and fired back, popping off half a dozen rounds in a semicircle.

On my knees again, I crawled into the undergrowth, which turned out to be a prickly bush. Spiny twigs ripped at my hair and clothing as I wriggled through and out the other side. My sight adjusted to the darkness; I saw stars almost hidden by cloud, a pale moon and the surrounding trees and undergrowth. I lunged to my feet and ran.

Royal found me in a little pine cave formed by the drooping branches of a big old tree. When he hissed, "Tiff?" and crept in beneath the branches, I was up on my knees aiming at him. I lowered the Ruger with an internal sigh of relief.

"They're gone. We can go back to the cabin."

"You're positive?"

"I would know if they were still here."

I signaled for him to go ahead and crawled out after him. I staggered upright. "Thanks for protecting me," I told him sarcastically.

Royal looked disheveled. He combed his fingers through his long hair, pushing it back over his shoulders. Then he stepped up to me and pulled me into his arms. "Thank the Lady you are safe," he said, and kissed me.

I fought the power of his kiss. I had to fight damn hard, and I managed to extricate myself and smack him in the chest with both hands, shoving him back a couple of paces. "If you'd arrested them. . . ."

"There were more than two people."

I started off, stopped. "Gee, thanks. Nice to know more than two of your people are targeting me." I peered about. "Which way?"

He indicated the direction with one hand. I indicated he should lead the way with a sweep of *my* hand. I followed him as he went in the opposite direction I would have taken.

"They *were* your people, right?" I asked in a low voice.

"Yes. And you were right, I should have arrested those two. I am truly sorry."

I watched where I put my feet. "Sorry doesn't cut it, mister." I felt through my hair, pulling out splinters, thankful none of them pierced my scalp.

"I told you, you need protection. The only reason you are with me now is while you raced through this. . . ," he angrily threw a hand out at the surrounding forest, ". . . this jungle, I removed most of them."

I stopped walking. "Most of them? Did your super-duper sensing thing tell you how many were here?"

He thrust his hands deep in his pockets and calmly told me: "Five. Two got away."

My mouth gaped. I closed it with a snap of my teeth. "You took out *three?* And what do you mean by *removed?*"

He got moving again. "Better you do not know."

I jogged behind him, trying to keep up with his long strides. "Sure it's better I don't know a thing when a hunter digs up a body here and there. What *were* you—?"

"Which is why I did not kill them. But I hurt them," I heard him say.

I knew he would not tell me more. As we walked back to the cabin through the silent forest, boots crunching on pine-needles, forest mulch and twigs turned brittle in the cold, questions buzzed through my mind. Why were the demons trying to kill me? Because I could identify them? Because I was useless to them if I couldn't tell them where Lawrence was, and therefore, in their opinion disposable? Because they didn't want me to find him? If Royal and the other demons were cohorts, why didn't he take advantage of the times we were together to get rid of me?

The cabin door was open. I ran for it and burst inside. The single room was empty.

"They took Mac!" I wailed.

"I think I left the door open."

"You what!" I gasped.

"I'm sorry. I'm not used to dogs. I did not think."

I turned around and screamed at him. "You moron! You lost my dog!"

Mac was a good distance from the cabin when Royal and I found him. Emboldened by Royal's assertion the shooters were long-gone, I called out Mac's name aloud. I was almost in tears. I could brave muggers, I could even put up a good front against demons, but the thought of my little dog lost and alone in the backcountry would likely destroy me.

Mac didn't yelp out his location and gratefully leap into my arms, panting little doggy kisses all over my face. We found him by the sheer volume of noise he made as he rooted and bumbled through the undergrowth. I thrashed through prickly gorse to reach him, hugged his heavy little body tight, and he *growled* at me! There's gratitude for you. He was not happy to be dragged back to civilization.

And drag him I had to. I'd left his leash in the car and I couldn't carry him far—he weights too much—and I didn't dare take Royal up on his offer to carry Mac. So I walked to the cabin kind of hunched over with my hand on Mac's collar. I thought I would never get upright again.

I put Mac in the backseat of the Subaru, put the shutters down over the cabin's windows and secured them, and locked the door. Then I poured lye down the hole in the outhouse and engaged the padlock on the door. All the while, Royal circled the cabin like a big, watchful cat.

I led the way in the Subaru, Royal coming behind in his new truck. As I drove down Pineview Canyon, I wondered what he did to those three men. He hurt them, he said. Did he hurt them bad? Did I care? Hell no. I hoped he hurt them bad enough they had second thoughts about coming after me again.

He took out three demons to save little old me. Of course, as an officer of the law, he would do it for anyone.

A few houselights still glowed as I pulled in my driveway, my neighbors watching late night movies. The Frankie's were away and their teens were having a party; loud music, young voices shouting and swearing. As I got out of the car, a youngster stumbled through the Frankie's front door and fell on his knees on their front lawn, and vomited. *Great.* The little hooligans would likely keep me up all night.

Royal's truck pulled up at the curb and stopped, engine purring. The headlights glared in my face as I crossed to my front door. I knew he would wait till I got inside the house.

I put my key in the lock and got the door open just a crack, and Mel's voice screeched at me: "It was them!"

"Look what they did!" Jack cried out.

Holding onto Mac's leash, I kicked the door all the way open.

Holy cow.

The coat-rack lay on the floor, part of the frame broken. My shoes were in the kitchen doorway. The small table where I kept my keys, wallet and whatever had been demolished. My only picture—two bull-moose facing off, with a backdrop of pines—lay against the wall with a cracked frame, the glass in shards. Clothes were all over the stairs.

"It was the demon, the one who came here, and another with red and black hair," Mel wailed.

"They trashed the place," I murmured. My gaze kept going back to the same things: the table, the coat-rack, the picture, then back again. I slowly pulled my gun.

Then Royal's arm went over my shoulders and hugged. It felt really nice, comforting, and I forgot for a moment he shouldn't hold me, and I should not let him.

The anger came suddenly, like acid erupting up my throat. I shrugged out from beneath his arm. "Your guys did this. Those fucking friends of yours you didn't arrest."

His face looked like thunder as he took in the damage, and I could tell he kept his tone level only with effort. "Why would you think so? And please stop calling them my guys."

A little sanity returned to tell me I should watch what I said. "I don't have anything worth stealing. They know I took something from Lindy's place and came looking for it."

"Breaking and entering is not always about theft. It's how some get their kicks."

I knew that. Didn't make me feel any better. And I knew what he did not: those two demons definitely went through my house.

He looked in the kitchen, and thumped the frame so hard with his closed fist the thing shuddered and I thought it would crack.

"Way to go. It's not enough my house is wrecked, you want to bring it down around my ears," I said dryly as I walked past him into the kitchen and saw the chaos in there.

He looked at his fist, moved it from the frame and uncurled his fingers.

"You need to leave now," I said suddenly as the damage all but overwhelmed me. Others might want someone with them at a time like this, not me. I needed to be alone, or as alone as Jack and Mel would let me.

He stood in the kitchen doorway with one hand braced on the frame. "I think I—"

"No. You should go. I don't want you here."

He eyed me intently, a small frown marring the bronzed skin of his brow. He nodded. "But I'm going to call it in, Tiff."

My mouth tightened. "I think that's my decision."

He loomed over me. "I'm a police officer. My duty is to report a break-in."

I perked one eyebrow. "Like it's your duty to report what happened at Monchard?"

His mouth went so tight I thought his lips might break his teeth, then he said, "If you expect me to say touché, think again."

I watched from the window to make sure he did leave, but he pulled over at the Frankie's house. I don't think he knocked, he went straight inside. A few minutes later youngsters came out as if the Pied Piper of Hamlin led them, swarming down the street like a horde of greasy rats. He came out last with three teen boys in tow. I expect they were too inebriated to make their own way home. He stuffed two in the back seat of the truck and the third in the front passenger seat, slammed the door, got in the driver's side and slammed that door, and the big red truck disappeared over the brow of the hill.

Chapter Thirteen

Where I live, high on the east bench, clouds often wreathe my house. Out of town visitors and particularly out of state visitors talk about the fog, but it is not fog. This high, you walk in the clouds.

Mike didn't phone this time. He came in person, looming out of the cloud bank, stepping up on my front porch. While I knew it boded no good, I reflected it was nice to have a *human* male come through my door for a change.

MacKlutzy growled a welcome.

Mike ignored Mac as the small dog hovered, eying Mike's ankles. A lot of people underestimate Scottish terriers; they don't know the little monsters have teeth like Rottweiler's. I kept a wary eye on my stubby buddy.

Mike stood in the hall. "Redecorating?"

He had been in my house only once before, but he noticed a difference. It must be a cop talent. I made a face at the hall. "Threw out a load of junk."

"It looks more . . . spacious," he agreed. He went in my small, rather gloomy living room, which seemed a more appropriate setting than my kitchen for what could be a solemn conversation.

I was exhausted from being up all night putting the house to rights. Everything breakable in the kitchen, they broke. I couldn't walk through without stepping on the remains of something. You cannot imagine the mess, and in the pantry. Perhaps they ran out of steam when they hit the upstairs. They smashed my monitor, turned my bureau over and pulled out every drawer in the three bedrooms. They tossed everything in my closet all over the room and down the staircase. But they didn't ruin my clothes, blankets or linens.

I swept up the remains, filling a dozen big plastic trash bags, and kept the washing machine and tumble dryer going all night.

People speak of feeling violated when their home is invaded and their property destroyed. I can understand this, because the destruction is unnecessary, an act of vandalism and vindictiveness. But it's not as if someone laid hands on their bodies. I didn't take having my things destroyed lightly—a few times during the night I got so angry I wanted to throw something myself—but nothing had sentimental value and the rest could be replaced.

I happened to look through the upstairs landing window at two in the morning, and spotted a big pickup parked way down the street. It was there every time I checked thereafter, but gone when the sun broached the mountain peaks.

Mike stood in the middle of the room with hands plunged deep in pants pockets, as if studying the décor, but I knew he was giving himself time. I let him take in the small wood-burning stove in its brick alcove, the faux-paneled walls, the mangy old flocked wallpaper and the few pieces of old but solid furniture. The small bay window didn't permit much light and turning on a lamp wouldn't help much.

Jack hung over my shoulder. "This does not look good."

I agreed. I think, from what I told Jack about the Lieutenant, he knew Mike almost as well as I did, and he correctly read Mike's posture. The man was unhappy and uncomfortable. I perched on the arm of the overstuffed couch. "Okay, Mike, give."

He kneaded his chin and looked at me sidelong. "You're not going to like it."

I made a noise in the back of my throat. "Let me see. You come to my house instead of phoning. You stand here looking like it's the last place you want to be. You tell me I'm not going to like it. What a surprise."

He pulled in a reluctant breath through pursed lips, blew it out, and looked down at me. "I want you to see if you can get anything from the other victims."

"What victims?" Had I missed something? Did we have another murder case on our hands?

"The bodies we could recover. The children."

My heart plummeted to my gut and sat like a lump of cold oatmeal.

I shook my head. "Nu-uh. You put me on looking for Lawrence. No mention of me and dead children."

"His disappearance and these others, they *have* to be linked. Sure, a tiny percentage of the missing children sharing the same birthday could be coincidence, but too many were born on the same day. This is massive, Tiff. We *will* put a stop to it. I'll use any advantage we have."

"Like me." I worried at my lower lip with my teeth. "What about Lawrence? He's more than just a case, Mike. He's a little boy in deep trouble."

"We're not giving up on him, Tiff."

I wished I could offer a solid excuse to refuse Mike. Having to talk to children . . . it would be tough. Mike didn't know what speaking to a dead child did to me.

But although I protested, I didn't really have a choice. I could see no way out. *Nope, I'm not going to help you solve your multiple abduction case. I'm not going to help you discover who murdered little boys.* No more cases would come my way. My only income would be gone, along with my reputation. Not to mention my self-esteem.

"Mike, I doubt you realize how . . . painful trying to talk to dead children can be," I offered. I realized, too late, I said *talk,* but he didn't notice.

His eyebrows almost met as he frowned. "I never thought about it."

"And they don't communicate well. When they're so young, and afraid, they have little or no composure. All we'd probably get would be something like 'it was a big man with black hair,' if we're lucky." I offered him a weak smile. "But if you really want me to try, of course I will. I just don't think it will help."

He rubbed the back of his neck, rolled his shoulders. He looked as tired as I felt. "How about we check out a couple. Colorado and Wyoming, right in our backyard. We could do it in a day."

"This close? My god!"

"This close, Tiff. Practically all around us."

So I agreed, pointless as I felt the exercise would be.

"Tomorrow morning, bright and early. You, me and Roy. First stop Saratoga, then on to Granby if we have to."

"Were they killed at the scene?"

"We don't know."

Great.

I was not looking forward to it. Not one tiny bit.

I drove down to the credit union after Mike left and withdrew two hundred dollars from my savings account. Two hundred buys a lot from the Salvation Army Thrift Shop.

Leaving Mac grumbling on the other side, I latched the gate and walked through the trees to the apartment block. I ambled along with hands deep in my pockets, thinking about relationships. About *my* relationships.

I had not had many.

I had always been solitary. My first memories are of a Division of Child and Family Services children's shelter, only the state-run agency had a different name back then. When I was eleven, my caseworker told me a groundskeeper found me on the steps of a Presbyterian church on a hot July night. My cute little wicker basket was actually a dog bed. My blanket and clothing were made in Canada. Was I born in Canada? Did my parent or parents come all the way to Providence, Utah, to dump me?

I don't remember all the foster care placements. I can think back to when I was maybe two, but nothing beforehand. They were not good places. There were always a lot of other children and the foster parents were more interested in the money they got from the state than caring for their charges. I kept to myself as much as I could because I just didn't like being with people. I left Utah before I was legal.

In Omaha, Nebraska, I worked fast-food restaurants. In Iowa, it was telemarketing. In South Dakota, an auto dealership. I worked as a field surveyor for an oil company in Wyoming for a year. I attended an office occupations school in Minnesota and got a secretarial job at the headquarters of a software manufacturer. Then I found myself at Lake Superior. Canada.

Did something inside want the parents I never knew? Did my subconscious lead me? I couldn't bear to think I unconsciously craved a family who didn't want me, so I skedaddled out of there and ended up in San Francisco, and stayed six years.

Then, pow! I could see dead people. No fanfare. No blast of lightning. Just that first confusing, scary moment when I stood outside the Sun and Bun café and spoke to a person nobody else saw. And I had no idea why.

My interest in my parents resurfaced. It seemed important to know if one or both had my talent. Did they know I had it? Is that why they dumped me? But there was no trail to follow. I gave up on them all over again.

But I would track them down one day, and maybe they could tell me why I saw dead people.

I didn't have friends; I had friendly acquaintances. I had two boyfriends before Colin, but I was not in love with them. I wasn't in love with Colin.

I knew Lindy was not at her apartment when I stepped inside, but I went from room to room anyway. The bedrooms were bare of furniture now and small pieces of trash littered the floors. The manager had started cleaning out the place. The air felt dead and fusty. The place seemed lonelier than ever and as I stood in the living room, so did I.

I was on the helipad when the copter landed. Mike and Royal joined me and we ducked and ran for the copter bent over, the downdraught from the rotors whipping my braid. Mike sat up front with the pilot; Royal and I climbed in back and buckled in. I watched the roof of Clarion PD recede, then we flew over Clarion and climbed to clear the eastern peaks.

I was still mad at Detective Royal Mortensen and pretended to ignore him, but those kisses intruded in my thoughts, the memory of them a feather-light pressure on my lips. A couple of times I stopped my fingers going up to brush them. I dozed as the copter headed for Wyoming, jerking awake each time I felt my head nod in the direction of his shoulder.

I know Wyoming well, cities big and small and the vast stretches of empty land between them. I've also spent long, happy days in the Rocky Mountains of Colorado. Ironically, not only had I visited both Saratoga, Wyoming and Granby, Colorado, they numbered among my favorite places to be.

I passed through Saratoga when driving home through Wyoming one summer, and the old western buildings on East Bridge Street, where it dissects the I-130, beckoned to me. I had to check them out. I thought I would take an hour to wander up and down East Bridge Street and discover what was inside those buildings, and ended up staying the entire day. I spent over an hour chatting with shopkeepers and town folk in every little shop I entered. I ate lunch at Lollipops and went back later in the afternoon for another helping of their delicious homemade ice-cream. I rented a motel room for the night and started out again the next morning.

In fact, I daydreamed of one day living in Saratoga, a tiny old western town out in the middle of nowhere with a population of fewer than 1,800, where people are friendly and traffic in the old part of town so sparse you don't bother to check for cars before you cross the road. And no lingering murder victims.

Of course, when I fell in love with Saratoga, it was the city; I did not explore the surrounding countryside. As we flew over Saratoga, the Hot Springs and the great North Platte River, I wondered if the spirit of a dead child lingered among the sagebrush below, and I said good-bye to my dream.

Ten miles outside Saratoga, we settled down at the Harley B Ranch on their personal pad. A little Cesna poked its nose out between the open doors of a small hangar. In states like Wyoming, where ranchlands are vast, ranchers often have their own planes. But since when did ranch houses become mansions? This place was a huge adobe concoction with red-tiled roof and balconies everywhere.

The rancher came out of the house to meet us; a tall, gangling, mahogany-skinned man named Andy Ferrin. After handshakes all around, he told us to follow him to his Jeep. He was a man of few words, or perhaps he didn't care to talk too much about finding a murdered child on his property. He must have gone over it with various law-enforcement agencies countless times when one of his hands found the body in the summer of 2006.

Mike climbed in front with Ferrin, which left me in back with Royal.

Despite my calf-length down coat, I just about froze until the heater kicked in. I took possession of the two blankets on the seat, wrapped one around my shoulders and put the other over my knees. We drove along a snow- and ice-packed trail heading west from the landing pad. Traffic must have used it regularly, or it would be hidden beneath the snow like the surrounding terrain. Rounding a small hill, suddenly we were in the middle of nowhere. Mountain ranges surrounded us, but they were far away. The landscape looked like a white desert where the merciless Wyoming winds had blown the snow into dunes. Some areas were under several feet, while in others, where the wind bared it, wiry grass and sagebrush poked up through. Fencing intersected the land in the distance, but nothing else broke the monotony.

Royal sat a bit too close for my comfort and I thought the heat between us had nothing to do with the way I was bundled up against the chill. Ahead of us, in the distance, a small stationary figure stood near the trail.

The Jeep bombed along and Ferrin made no effort to avoid potholes. Or perhaps he couldn't miss so many.

We approached the person near the trail and indeed he stood at the very edge: a small elderly man in a heavy, knee-length overcoat of undeterminable color, baggy gray pants and beat up old boots, a hemp sack slung over one shoulder. He wore a hat like I owned, the one I used in extra cold temperatures, with earflaps, except his looked filthy. Wisps of gray hair straggled from beneath it.

Ferrin didn't slow and I felt sorry for the old guy who stood motionless in the bitter cold. As we drove past him, I grinned apologetically and waved my hand. He gave me a gap-toothed leer in return.

Yes, definitely a leer.

Royal's gaze bore into me. I frowned at him. "What?"

"What were you waving at?"

Oh, crap!

Chapter Fourteen

Mike twisted to face us. "Something wrong, Tiff?"

"No. No. A fox. Saw a fox. I happen to like waving at foxes. Cute little things. Smile and wave, it's what I do when I see a fox. They appreciate it," I babbled.

Not the smartest thing to say, because I knew I had to talk to the old fellow when we drove back to the ranch. My garbled explanation was for Ferrin's benefit, but he looked at me in the rear-view mirror like I was crazy. I gave him a weak smile.

I laid my head back on the seat and closed my eyes. I didn't want to see anything else before we reached our destination.

The Jeep pulled up at a snow break not long after. The site lay near the property line close to I-130, and I had a feeling I would not find anything.

I went through the motions; got out of the Jeep and looked around; stood like a statue as if trying to sense something.

I sighed and turned to Mike. "Nothing. Sorry."

Mike paced to the snow break, turned back to face me. "Are you sure? Maybe you need a little longer."

"I'm sure, Mike. I don't need a minute more."

Mike scowled, but trudged past me to the Jeep. I rejoined Royal in the back seat. I looked at the desolate landscape, imagining a tiny body crumpled near the fence. It killed me to know *children* were out there, lost and alone. Did they realize, at their young age, what happened to them?

Ferrin strapped on his seat belt. "So it could be my property was a convenient place to drop the boy. The killer could have come from anywhere."

"True," from Mike.

Ferrin nodded to himself. "Good. When we found him on my land, I thought maybe someone local did it."

Royal didn't reassure him. "That could still be the case, Mr. Ferrin."

Ferrin *harrumphed* and we drove off.

The little old man showed up ahead of us not many minutes later. I swore beneath my breath. Much as I would have liked to, I couldn't ignore him. When we were fifty feet away, I asked Ferrin to pull over. He swiveled his eyes at me but didn't slow. I figured he wanted my reason to stop.

"Something happened here," I told Mike.

He got that *here we go again* expression, but didn't argue. He asked a puzzled Ferrin to pull up.

Royal put his mouth near my ear. "So it was not a fox. One of your ghosts?"

With a nod, I edged away. Keeping one blanket around my shoulders, I stepped from the Jeep and tottered the rest of the way. The rancher turned off the engine.

The chill ate at my exposed skin. It must have been fifteen degrees, balmy compared to what temperatures would be by February. I watched where I put my feet; the tracks made by the Jeep were already icing over.

The old guy stood only a tad above five feet tall and I didn't want to loom over him, but he might be insulted if I treated him like a child and bent over, or squatted. So I stood on the other side of the track across from him. "Hello."

A woman stood just about where I was. Mid-thirties at a guess, long auburn hair, small green eyes, fleshy cheeks, pouting lips, a tight blue dress which left nothing to the imagination, she distracted him while another person reached from behind and sawed at his throat. He wasn't afraid—a little puzzled why they took him out to the middle of nowhere, but otherwise pretty much enjoying himself. The attack came as a shock, quick but messy. No time to struggle; he was old and weak and they were strong.

I had seen many expressions on a ghost's face, but not a permanent leer. Leering, he lifted one hairy, gnarled hand to touch the side of his hat. "Howdy,"

Howdy? How long had he been out here?

"How come you're out in the middle of nowhere? What happened to you?" I asked, although I already knew.

He raised his whiskered chin, at the same time pulling down the neck of his dirty shirt to reveal a jaggedly gashed throat. "Stinkin' nephew, Missy. Slit me throat, he did, the dirty bastard. And the knife was notched. God Almighty it hurt."

"Oh, I'm sorry. Why did he do it?"

He rubbed at his whiskers. "Me money, no doubt. Don't believe in them banks. Never did. Every cent I earned, I kept close to home."

"He was your heir?"

"Could've been. Never made a will. Suppose he were me nearest livin' kin." He stamped one foot. "Dang it! If I'd knowed what a sneakin' little black-hearted bastard he was, I'd've left everything to the dog pound!"

I folded my arms over my chest to keep the blanket in place, cocked my head on one side. "Who was with your nephew?"

He pulled on one earlobe. "How d'ya know that?"

"You were ogling someone and I don't think it was your nephew."

"Was Avril, his wife. Face like the side of a barn but titties like a couple of melons. Always fallin' out her dress."

"What's your name?"

He peered at me with watery blue eyes. "Jeremiah."

"Jeremiah what?"

"Johnson."

I slowly clapped my hands. "Bravo. What's your real name?"

"Henry. Henry Randall."

"And your nephew's name?"

His tone turned suspicious. "Why you askin' all these questions, Missy. An' how come you see me when no one else can?"

"It's what I do, Henry. What's more, I'll do my best to bring your nephew to justice."

"Oh, aye? That'd be nice." He ran his tongue over his lips. "I'll tell you what'd be nicer, though."

I forestalled him. "I can't do anything about you being stuck out here. I'm really sorry, but I can't. You will pass on eventually, Henry."

"Nah, not that! Show me yer titties."

"My. . . ?"

His permanently twitched-back lips allowed me the full glory of his almost toothless mouth. "Haven't seen a gal's titties for a good long time. Not since Avril. Jest open up yer shirt, jest a flash, like. That'll do me. Looks like you got a good pair on you."

I spluttered. "Henry!"

"Forget it, then. How 'bout you come over here and let me have a feel."

I sobered. "You can't, Henry, and I bet you know already."

"Tarnation! This is me fate, then? Standin' here in the middle of Wyomin' on me lonesome?"

"Not if we can get your nephew the death penalty."

He sagged. "An' that's likely, ain't it."

I hugged the blanket tighter around me as I began to shiver. "Did he leave your body out here?"

"Oh, aye." He stamped his foot again. "Right here, 'neath me."

I looked about, but couldn't see anything to mark the spot. "Okay, Henry, I'm going to the Jeep, but I'll be back in a minute."

He nodded, somehow making his leer seem glum, or perhaps it was my imagination.

I tromped back to the Jeep. Mike and the rancher were having an obviously animated conversation, probably about the crazy consultant.

I stopped at the driver's side. Ferrin rolled down the window.

"Mr. Ferrin, have you got anything heavy which I could use as a marker?"

Ferrin glanced at Mike. "Uh, the spare tire, I guess."

"What's going on, Tiff?" Mike asked.

"Does the name Henry Randall ring a bell?" I asked the rancher.

He squinted one eye. "Sure. Old Henry was an eccentric. Spent most of his days and evenings walking through town, bothering the ladies."

I bet I knew how.

"But he was harmless," Ferrin concluded.

"Was?" Royal asked from the back seat.

"Disappeared two years ago. Unfortunately, we didn't realize till someone reported they hadn't seen him for a couple of weeks. We launched a search, but never found a trace of the old guy. Had the habit of walking out in the desert, we reckon he passed away out here and the animals took care of him. He was eighty-five and in poor health."

I was fast becoming frozen. I got in the back seat with Royal and asked Ferrin to drive on. When we reached old Henry, I asked the rancher to stop.

Mike and Royal unfastened the Jeep's spare tire and laid it by the trail at Henry's feet. Henry watched them, leering forlornly.

I waited till they got back in the Jeep. "Get a team out and dig here, and you'll find Henry Randall's body."

Looking at the spot, Mike spoke to Ferrin. "Spread the word to your hands, do not move that tire."

Ferrin looked at Mike, at the tire, at me in the rear view mirror. "She's saying Henry's buried here?"

"He is," I told him. "Can we get back to the ranch now, please?"

We started off. As we passed Henry, I winked at him. "Does Henry's nephew still live around here?"

"Billy Norris? He moved to Rawlings when we couldn't find Henry. Nice guy. He donated the old house to the Saratoga Historic Society. Had to do some restoration, Henry never took care of the place."

Mike caught on. "You hear anything of him?"

"He opened his own car dealership."

"Did he inherit anything from Henry, apart from the house?" I asked.

"Not a cent. Henry was a pauper. He would've starved to death if not for handouts from the community."

I leaned forward to speak to Mike. "I think if you look into it, you'll find Norris didn't get a loan to start his business, he used cold, hard cash. Henry's cash."

"Mr. Ferrin," Royal interjected, "you realize this is now a police investigation and this conversation goes no farther."

The rancher puckered his brow. "You think Henry had money and Billy took it? So? Billy has a legal right to Henry's estate."

I exchanged looks with Mike and he gave me the okay with a nod. "He did more than take Henry's money. He took Henry's life," I said.

Ferrin brought the Jeep to a stop and twisted in his seat to look at me. "You're out of line, lady. Billy wouldn't harm a hair on that old man's head. He didn't murder his uncle."

"I know he did; he and his wife."

"And you know this because. . . ?"

I drew my shoulders up to my ears. "Henry told me."

Chapter Fifteen

———ϒ———

I waited for Royal to start in with the questions. Mike was way past the *how do you know, are you sure, how can you tell, you must be mistaken* stage, but it took years, and although Royal had worked with psychics and mediums, he hadn't worked with me. But he didn't say a word as we climbed back in the copter. Maybe Mike warned him I won't discuss how I get information from the dead.

I laid my head back on the cushioned headrest and closed my eyes. The tension in my body began to ease. After Granby, I could go home and concentrate on finding Lawrence.

But what about Lindy? Where was she? Had she already passed over? This case was so not typical of anything I experienced before.

"Tired, Tiff?" Royal asked. His hand came down gently on the back of mine.

I didn't have the energy to free myself, and anyway, his fingers warmed my cold skin.

I vacationed in a condo in Granby for a week one summer. Just me and Mac.

We took long walks on the trails near the ski lifts and I think we both lost a little weight. We investigated tiny Granby and the larger city of Winter Park, drove through the Rocky Mountain National Forest and over the Rockies to Estes Park. We walked the old main street of Grand Lake and ate a picnic in the park, then I sat on the edge of the lake for an hour, looking at the water and persuading Mac not to jump in after the mallard.

A small city of 1,500 people in the Colorado Rocky Mountain valley, a valley devoted to tourism—holiday homes, apartments and condos everywhere—Granby itself doesn't have a lot to offer to a big-city dweller, but I like it and its proximity to the Rocky Mountains makes it a good base for sightseeing. Prices in the small stores and one small supermarket are outrageous, but the local people are unpretentious and friendly.

As Mike, Royal and I walked past the bakery, the skies above Granby were clear and blue and the pale winter sun beat down thinly. Snow already coated the Rocky Mountain peaks. An early influx of skiers and snowboarders crowded the small town, taking a look before they got down to the serious business of tackling the slopes.

Granby was different. I felt him as we neared the liquor store. I heard him, a nonsense rhyme in a soft, whispering sing-song voice. He was singing as he died. I stopped, inexplicably chilled, and clasped the collar of my jacket closer to my neck.

"Are you getting something?" Mike asked as he peered at me.

"Where is he?" I rasped as I reminded myself, for the umpteenth time, Mike did not know what I heard and felt right then.

Mike indicated the mouth of an alley just head of us. It ran between two unoccupied buildings which were small, square and identical, of faded and weathered blue clapboard, each with one big window in front. We walked on.

"How old was he?"

"Five and a half," Mike said.

"His name?"

"Charles Geary. Parents called him Charlie."

I straightened up, sucking in my gut, and started along the alley.

Narrow, unpaved, it smelled strongly of cat urine. Doors to the buildings either side faced each other across the alley and a few empty, battered garbage cans lay on their sides. Twenty feet down, on the right, a metal staircase went up the side of a building to the first floor. Charlie waited up there, somewhere behind the peeling door

I trudged up the steps like I climbed to my doom. I wished the staircase were a hundred miles long. I wished I didn't have to talk to the child and let him know yes, someone saw him and no, I couldn't help him. Mike and Royal followed me up.

A Realtor's lockbox padlocked the door. Mike punched in the code to open the box and got out the key. He opened the door and stood aside to let me enter.

I walked inside the living room of a small, bare, cold apartment.

I followed Charlie's voice to his bedroom. He sat cross-legged on the bare board floor, so small, and wearing his blue PJs with green-faced Incredible Hulks all over them. The PJs were a little grubby and damp in the crotch. Shoulder-length hair as pale as mine wisped over his pale-blue eyes and framed his downy cheeks. He looked up as I walked toward him, but his body language didn't indicate interest. He didn't think I could see him.

He didn't know to be afraid of them. He sat on the floor playing with his toys, humming his song. Someone approached him and he looked up, a half-smile on his face, still humming. A hand flicked out, a silver blade flashed.

The man was there and gone in a second. A demon moving at more than human speed. I did not get a fix on his face, but Charlie saw him with the uncanny perception of those about to die.

I squatted down in front of Charlie. I kept my voice low so Royal and Mike would hear only a murmur. With luck they would think I muttered psychic-style gibberish. "Hello, Charlie."

He looked at me, and as most children do, came right to the point. "Nobody else can see me."

I hunched my shoulders. "Do you know why, Charlie?"

He shook his head. "No. When will Mom and Dad be home?"

My heart cracked. So maybe I didn't feel an actual, physical crack, but I knew it was cracking and there would be a gaping hole by the time I finished. "Not yet. But you'll be with them again one day."

"When? Will it be soon?"

"I don't know, Charlie. But if we find the man who hurt you, you can go to a place where you won't be alone while you wait for them." I hoped.

Charlie frowned, but accepted that without question. "Oh," he said, "it was him."

"What do you mean, Charlie? I'm the only one here."

He pointed toward the door. "No, him, over there."

I looked back over my shoulder, hoping to see a third person, but only Mike and Royal stood at the door. Royal gave me what I took to be an encouraging smile. Mike looked at his feet.

"What does he look like?"

Charlie still pointed. "The big man with the long funny-looking hair," he insisted.

I felt as if the air had been sucked out of me. I squatted for a good fifteen seconds while Charlie looked up at me and my mind whirled. Royal Mortensen killed those boys. He killed little Charlie Geary.

I shuddered in a breath and gave myself a mental shake. I had to handle this right.

"Charlie, I'm going to ask those men to come here so you can see them better. Then if you still think it's him, you give me a nod."

Charlie's solemn little face went back to Royal. "I *know* it was him."

The dead never forget the face of their killer.

"Please, Charlie. . . ."

"Oh, okay."

So I beckoned to Mike and Royal, and they came in the room to stand just behind me. I watched Charlie's face as his gaze lifted to Royal, and he nodded.

I will never forget the look on Mike's face when I told him. We went outside and yelled at each other for a while, and I was surprised to find Royal still waiting when we got back to him. He must have heard us. He could have lit out, but he waited.

Mike didn't read Royal his rights or cuff him, but he asked for his badge and gun while they "sorted it out." Both looked numb. No—Royal didn't look numb, he looked very deep in thought, and Mike looked defeated.

Chapter Sixteen

———♈———

I walked into my house with my head down. As I said, I learned to control any outward reflection of my emotions long ago and I think Mike saw only anger and exasperation, but I'd wanted to cry since leaving him and Royal at the PD.

The worst of it? I didn't want it to be Royal. I didn't want him to be the murderer, the one who personally did the job. I know, when I met him I made that assumption, but something changed. I was attracted to him, dammit! He was gorgeous and enigmatic and . . . and he had a kind of presence which turned me inside out.

Some part of me didn't wanted Royal to be a bad guy.

"What's wrong, Sweetie?" Mel asked.

"Nothing!" I stomped past her and up the stairs to my bedroom, shut the door and threw myself on the bed.

This must be the worst day of my life. Finding little Charlie, learning Royal was the killer, having to leave poor Charlie alone again, sitting in an empty, dirty, lonely apartment in his Incredible Hulk PJs.

If God would grant me one boon, I would ask if I could gather up all the little lost shades and put them together in one place, so they would not be lonely while they waited to pass over.

I buried my face in the pillow.

I sat in the kitchen with Lawrence's file on the table and tried to put Royal out of my mind. I couldn't do it. Was the PD carrying out an investigation on one of their own? What did the division think of me pointing the finger at him?

Most of them would pooh-pooh my accusation. A lot of them would be mad at me. But Mike believed me, just as on the other cases in which I participated, and that must count for something.

I frowned at the manila folder. But the case wasn't like the others I helped out on, except in one way: Mike initially had only my word to go on. Royal was one of theirs. Would Mike put the same pressure on his detective as he did the other suspects I fingered?

Oh hell. Telling Mike was a huge mistake. He would not do a thing without proof, not in this instance, and what solid proof did he have Royal committed those murders? I should have kept my mouth shut and looked for evidence.

By telling Mike, I may have done nothing more than dig a big hole for myself.

I was driving myself crazy, one minute mourning the loss of a man who had never been mine, the next scared at the thought he'd be free to come after me. I shivered. *Think of something else, Tiff.* I opened the folder and spread the papers on the table.

"You look better this morning!" Mel said brightly.

I scowled at her.

"You and your big mouth," Jack told her.

They got in an argument and I tuned them out. I went over it again, everything I had on Lindy and Lawrence, my notes and copies of the police file. Nothing new jumped out at me.

I looked at Lawrence's drawing. Something about it nagged at me. Taking the drawing with me, I crossed the kitchen and rooted in what I call the trash drawer till I found my big magnifying glass.

The tall figure with yellow hair. It could be a tall man, with a smile on his face, a nice smile, not an evil scowl. Lawrence liked him. If the man frightened him, the boy would not put a smile on the guy's face. And right then a memory flitted through my mind, a memory of something I saw back in Lindy's apartment.

I dropped the magnifying glass on the counter.

I had to get back in there.

Because of Lawrence's disappearance and the removal of all evidence of him, the apartment was now designated a crime scene, but the manager remembered me and gave me the key. I went up the inner stairwell and let myself in Lindy's hall. I flicked on the light.

The apartment already had the neglected air a place gets when it has been empty for a while, and a stale, flat smell almost overrode the potpourri. I tore into the living room and heaved a silent sigh of relief when I saw the furniture still in there. I went directly to Lindy's roll-top desk and pulled the envelope I wanted from the second drawer down. I sorted through the papers inside, held one up before my face.

Oh. My. God.

I folded the piece of paper, tucked it in my pocket and headed for the front door. Someone stole away a little boy and I was pretty sure, now, I could identify that someone. The same someone touched Lindy, and I asked myself why. Did he know what I did for a living, did he want her to wander away from the scene of her death and come to me?

I dismissed the idea. He had no reason to send Lindy's shade to the local psychic, not when Lindy died of natural causes, and he had Lawrence. He touched Lindy for another reason. But why didn't matter one iota. I had to get the child back.

I needed backup. He could pull some Otherworldly trick on me if prepared to risk exposing his true nature, and if he turned nasty I would not stand a chance alone.

The light in the stairwell must have blown while I was in the apartment, but the outside light limned the arch at the bottom of the stairwell. Watching where I put my feet, I charged down the steps, at the same time flipping open my cell phone and punching in Mike's number. It rang five times, and I wondered if he sat at his desk looking at the caller ID on his phone, reluctant to take a call from me. But then he picked up.

"Mike, I think I know where Lawrence is!"

A second later something struck the back of my head and I fell.

I came awake with my chin on my breastbone. I couldn't see properly, just a blur. I frantically blinked my eyes, afraid the blow to the back of my head affected my vision, but it didn't help. I tried to rub them and couldn't move my hands.

My hands were tied to the arms of a chair.

Panic threatened to overwhelm me and I started to hyperventilate.

Something cold and wet hit me in the face. Another dose slapped me in the neck and chest and I realized I was naked. I gasped and spluttered and I got mad. "You son of a bitch," I began as my sight cleared.

Caesar sat across from me, a table between us.

For one stunned moment I just stared at him. Then, as anger burned through me, I bared my teeth and snarled something not to be repeated in polite company. He laughed at me.

I sat in an unpadded wingback chair, naked as the day I was born, spine aching from an upright position against an unyielding surface. Thick, coarse rope imprisoned my wrists tight to the chair arms. My head hurt and my scalp felt tight.

An empty glass jug sat on the table and I thought—hoped—the wet stuff on me was water from out of it.

I blinked a few times and looked around. We sat in gloom close to the wall of a vast, circular room which must have been one hundred feet in diameter. The wall looked like plaster, smooth, pale-gray and featureless, and curved up like the sides of a bowl to a vaulted ceiling perhaps fifty foot high in the center. A dozen or so shining yellow globes hung from long cables in a cluster, dropping down thirty feet; they provided adequate illumination to the middle of the room, but left the edges in shadow. The inside of an arched opening to the left of where I sat glowed blue, showing steps leading upward. My bare feet rested on a floor of dark, dirty, scarred hardwood.

I sat at the long side of a rectangular table made of pale wooden boards polished to a dull sheen, four foot by twelve at a guess, Caesar facing me on the opposite side. My chair was one of a matching dozen positioned around it, unoccupied but for me and the gold-haired demon. The grouping of table and chairs made a small island in what appeared to be an otherwise empty space, devoid of other furniture or any kind of ornamentation. It had the same ancient, empty feel of a cavern deep beneath the earth, or a huge catacomb minus bodies and bones. I inhaled dry, musty air through my nostrils.

The sheer size and barrenness of the surroundings intimidated me, but not as much as my helplessness in the hands of my enemies.

When I say empty, I don't mean empty of people. Caesar had a few friends with him, about thirty demons who stood in a semi-circle behind him. Demons of all heights and widths and hair coloring, demons with flashing eyes and pointed teeth, and I saw nothing friendly in their smiles. Their clothing was archaic: long, wide-sleeved shirts, embroidered tunics, tight hose, all a riot of metallic colors. Their narrow feet were bare.

"Where is Lawrence Marchant?" Caesar drawled.

I opened my mouth to rant at him, then pressed my lips together. I refused to give him anything.

He leaned over the table. "You were speaking on your telephone. You said you thought you knew Lawrence's location. You would do well to tell me."

I couldn't hold it in any longer. I yelled, "You bastard! You murdering bastard! What makes you think you'll get away with coming to *my* world and killing children?"

My voice created an echo in the cavernous place: *children, children,* it called back to me. The demons nearest us smiled, the white enamel of their teeth standing out in faces of pale metallic colors.

Caesar waved his hand back at his pals. "Oh, I had a little help."

I silently vowed to hold my tongue and Caesar said nothing more. Minutes ticked by. The demons were uncannily motionless now. I wished they would shuffle, or whisper, or move their heads, or anything rather than watch me with hungry, chaotic eyes. Was I still on Earth, or in Royal's world, his reality? How long had I been here? Panic fluttered in my chest.

I heard movement behind me and a hand fell on my shoulder. I flinched as I looked up. "Hello, Tiff," Royal said.

Relief so intense, so *wonderful*, settled over me, making me lightheaded. *Thank you, God. I will never take your name in vain again!* Royal was here. He had tracked me down. "Royal," I croaked.

"Hush now," he crooned. "It'll be okay."

He went behind me. Both hands on my shoulders now, fingers digging in my flesh, hurting. I felt his mouth on my hair, nuzzling, and he inhaled deeply. I couldn't see him where he stood behind the high back of the chair, but . . . it felt wrong.

It's Royal, I told myself. I looked at the demons. *He won't let them hurt me. He has a plan.*

He came from behind the chair, fingers trailing down my arm to the wrist, diagonally across my belly to my left thigh. His hand dipped to brush my pale pubic hair, making me gasp and clench my muscles. "Patience, my Tiffany. It will soon be over," he said in that same eerie croon. "All over."

My gut cramped. I looked ahead with blurring eyes, chilled by numbing disappointment as I realized how completely I let him dupe me. The man I thought I knew would howl with rage and tear my bonds to pieces with his bare hands. He would not stand next to me, his mouth on my hair, while ropes held me and a horde of demons watched. He would not touch me like that in front of an audience.

Royal had not come to save me. He was one of them.

He patted my shoulder and left me, and ambled around the table to Caesar. His arm shot out, his hand fastened on a thick hank of sun-gold hair and he hauled Caesar to his feet and to one side. "Get out of my chair."

Caesar staggered but kept his feet. His expression was murderous, yet he stepped back and made a bow from the waist down. "Forgive me, Lord."

Royal lounged in the chair, twirling a lock of hair in the fingers of his right hand. He wore a silken, billowing white shirt open to his navel, the long sleeves fastened at his wrists with sparkling studs. Gold and jewels sparkled in his ears and on his fingers and glinted in the copper-gold of his hair. Yesterday, I would have admired the smooth, hairless chest framed by rippling silk, the narrow hips and solid thighs beneath skintight gray hose. Now I saw only the curl to his lip, the disdain in his glowing brown eyes.

He smiled at me, revealing his pointed teeth.

So that was a lie, too.

As I watched his beautiful face, my fear melted away. There is no place for fear in a heart which seethes with rage. Rage at him for fooling me, at allowing myself to be duped. For being sucked in by his seductive ways. For being his victim. This was the man . . . I let him touch me and make me want more. I felt dirty.

I turned my face from him. I couldn't look at him anymore.

"Tiff, look at me," Royal said.

My voice was heavy with revulsion. "Tried it. Don't like what I see."

A hand snaked from behind the chair. An unseen demon's blunt-nailed fingers dug in the skin of my mouth and chin, and forced my head around. I closed my eyes.

"Don't make him open your eyes for you," Royal said.

I opened them, blinking, to see his pointed smile again. The hand of the unseen demon let me go. "How are you with torture?" Royal asked in a pleasant, even voice.

I felt my face blanch as his words sank in. The water on my body had nearly dried, but perspiration replaced it now. How was I with torture? I had no idea. I imagined I would scream my head off. But did he mean torture or torment, because to my mind the demon way of persuasion, the sexual desire they could arouse with just a touch would be as bad as physical pain when done by his hands. To be used so by Royal would be the ultimate humiliation. I would rather he stuck me with a knife.

I got my answer when he casually nodded to one of the demons near the table. This one's hair shimmered like brushed stainless-steel and pale eyes like gray ice glinted from pale pewter skin. He walked to me, pulled back his hand and cracked the side of my face hard and fast with his palm, a blow which took my breath and knocked my head to one side. My other cheek hit the wing of the chair and I yelped.

Oh, *that* kind of torture.

But I couldn't tell Royal where Lawrence was, not willingly. I was not brave, I didn't possess the proverbial nerves of steel, but I couldn't condemn a little boy to death at the hands of monsters. I would not be able to live with myself.

As I tried to lift my aching head, I spotted my clothes in a pile on the floor at the end of the table. My jewelry and the Ruger were on top. They had somehow managed to get it off me without burning themselves.

If only I could free myself. The gun could as well be a hundred miles away.

I tried to stoke my anger, but a sense of helplessness and betrayal overwhelmed everything else. I looked into the depths of the room again, my gaze running over Royal, his demon clan, the huge empty space beyond them. Nobody leapt out of the shadows to rescue me.

I slowly turned my head to face Royal. I looked him in his gleaming eyes. "I can't tell you anything."

A tiny smile ticked at his lips. "Are you sure? We could have a very pleasant relationship, you and I."

"In your dreams," I whispered.

"You would give your life for a child?"

My heart faltered, then pounded and the space around me started to fade. I thought I would throw up and pass out at the same time. *Yeah, choke to death on your own vomit and save him going to all that trouble killing you,* I thought inanely. Because I knew, whatever I told him, he would kill me anyway, as he killed those little boys. As he would kill Lawrence.

Nobody knows I'm here. No one is coming for me. I'll be stuck in this god-awful place till he dies. I'll be a missing person, then a cold case. Jack. Mel. What will they think when I don't come home, what will they feel? Will they go on their way when they figure out I'm never coming back? Will they hang on, till other people live in my house—it will give them something to look at. And Mac! Who will care for my boy, who will love the irritable little beast like I do? Please, someone, take him to Janie, don't put him in the pound.

A morass of want, need and regret spilled through me. But I would not send them to that little boy. I would do what I could to protect Lawrence; it was the only thing left to me. I hoped, if they hurt me, my mouth would not betray me.

I curled my hands and dug my nails in my palms till they stung. Then I met his eyes. "You won't learn where Lawrence is from me."

He spread his hands as if with regret. "So be it."

He nodded at a demon with hair the color of freshly shed blood and red jade eyes, who stood with muscular arms folded. The demon joined the silver-haired guy and moved to stand on the other side of me. Each worked on untying one of my wrists, the rope rasping my skin. Soon as I realized what they were up to, I got my feet planted firmly on the floor. I tried to ignore my aching face and back. I waited till both ties were undone and they started to haul me upright.

I wasn't going out without a fight.

I exploded from the chair, crooked my arm and elbowed the silver-haired demon in the face. My elbow caught his nose and he reeled back a step, clapping hands to face then grunting with pain as his fingers nudged his nose. I lunged at the table, plucked up the glass jug and swung to smash it in the other demon's face. He tried to duck out of the way, but I altered the trajectory and managed to break the glass against his ear.

I stumbled along by the table, heading for my gun, but the bloody-haired demon grabbed my arm from behind, spun me and pinned me to the edge of table. I spat in his face, and as he grinned through the saliva spotting his lips, brought up my knee. Hard.

He buckled, hands going to the offended area.

I took another step, but another demon got between me and my weapon. With a thin smile, he wagged an admonishing finger at me.

So I went for Royal. It was the least I could do. I jumped on the table and aimed a kick at his face. He caught my ankle, twisted it and flipped me over. I went down like a log, landing on my side on the hard wood; my sore face hit with a meaty thunk. Before I could move, they were on me.

Half a dozen of them hoisted me in the air; hands on my bare calves, thighs, buttocks, waist and back. My head hung down at a painful angle. A blue-haired demon walked ahead of us, pulling on my braid as if he led a recalcitrant animal. I thought my hair would tear free of my scalp.

We didn't go far, maybe twenty feet. The demons ahead of us parted to reveal a strange looking contraption low on the ground, something like a square, demon-sized platform made of thick lengths of wood put together like latticework. I had not seen it as I sat at the table with the demons blocking my view. It stuck up from the floor on an angle, so the top hung back farther than the base. They hoisted me higher with a kind of merry cheer, then lowered me none too gently to the platform.

Badly planed wood and splinters dug in my skin. Still short of breath after hitting the table, I didn't have strength left to struggle as they tied my wrists and ankles to the thing. It didn't support me well, and bits of me bulged through gaps, while the weight of my body pressed other parts into the rough wood.

The entire clan gathered en masse, one body of seething hair and glittering eyes.

They parted to let Royal through. He held a whip in one hand, a nasty-looking tool made of separate lashes, each tipped with a tiny piece of clear, sharp crystal.

I moaned aloud and wrenched my wrists about, instinctively trying to protect my body with my hands.

Royal gave the whip an experimental flick, and crystal sparked. He dipped his head and smiled cruelly.

The first stroke was gently done. He put little effort in it. The crystal seemed to lick my skin, then bit in my waist and one hip like shards of glass and I yelped.

I took air in through my nose, let it out slowly through my mouth, looked down at my body. The nicks made by the crystal were minuscule, but already they welled with blood. I imagined how I would feel after a score, fifty, a hundred, until my body became one piece of bloody meat.

One. You can do two.

He coiled the whip in, let it loose, snaked it through the air so the crystals glittered like ice and chimed like tiny bells.

The next stroke caught me across the shoulder and breasts. I cried out again, a high thin sound echoing and dying to a whimper.

Two. You can do three. Dammit, you can do it!

Blood trickled on my belly. He reined in the whip.

Chapter Seventeen

—♈—

As Royal raised his arm, a voice literally boomed through the huge room.

"I challenge you for the life of this woman!"

Head high, he lowered the whip and turned a slow circle. His mouth twisted in an ugly smile. "Ryel, you have no place here," he said softly, slowly.

The body of demons drew back, creating a path, and Royal walked through them. He stopped fifteen feet from . . . Royal?

The pain eradicated by sheer astonishment, I stared at Royal One with the whip in his hand, and Royal Two. Face to face, they were identical. *What the fuck?*

Royal One held very still, his body a single, tense line. "Leave while you still may," he growled.

Royal Two said nothing as he sternly regarded Royal One. All in black—tight jeans, button-up shirt, jacket and boots—he looked more like the Royal I was used to, but he held a sword in one hand, a long thing like a slim scimitar with a wicked curve at the end.

In an otherwise deathly silence, I could hear my heartbeat. The entire room seemed to throb with it.

"You intrude here," Royal One growled.

Royal Two's voice came low and harsh. "It is no intrusion when I come to claim what is mine. I offer challenge. Accept, or slither back to your hole."

They glared at each other, while the demon clan shuffled and whispered. Their voices rose, the buzzing of wasps, till I no longer heard the pounding of my heart. Royal One motioned with his hand and their speech abruptly cut off. Silence held the huge room once again, wrapping me like a cold hand.

Royal One nodded. "So be it."

Royal Two peeled off his jacket and slung it to one side. He clasped the hilt of the sword in both hands and raised it, assuming a martial stance, and every muscle bulged like an enraged bull's. His copper-gold hair spat sparks as it swirled about his head. His jaw was rigid, his expression thunderous.

He was larger than life. He was magnificent.

Wait a minute! Pointed teeth? So easy to summon the feel of Royal's mouth on mine. He didn't have pointed teeth.

Royal One was not *my* Royal.

The demon who was not Royal dropped his whip and lifted one hand. A sword flew through the air and he neatly caught it by the hilt, but did not lift it to meet Royal's challenge. He looked past the real Royal, to me, as a subtle change came over his face, and he was not quite Royal anymore. His build was slighter, his hair longer, his cheekbones sharper with hollows beneath them.

With only a flash of his eyes, the baring of pointed teeth as warning, he lunged at Royal. Royal caught the blade on his and they snarled in each other's faces over the crossed hilts. Then they broke apart as if by mutual consent and backed away.

The other demons moved back to give them space. Royal and the other guy slowly circled, blades resting on their shoulders, each studying the other's face. They darted in.

It was beautiful, in a lethal kind of way. All graceful strokes and weaving bodies. A dance. A deadly dance. Blades flicked and swung and parried as if separate entities from the men who wielded them. Bodies spun, ducked and swayed. Their feet seemed to barely touch the floor.

I don't know anything about fighting with a blade, but I quickly realized they were evenly matched. I didn't think one could overcome the other, until one of them tired. The clash of blades made an unholy racket, the sound amplified, clattering back and forth across the room as if a whole platoon fought.

With one eye on the combatants, a prayer for the real Royal in my heart, I worked on the ropes which bound me.

The demons completely enclosed the arena in which Royal danced. The size of the room gave them ample space in which to maneuver and as the two darted about, the demons flowed back away from them, then flowed in again, the motion of a huge, undulating snake. I watched them glide back and forth to give Royal and his opponent space to duel, and hoped they'd get splinters in their bare feet from the rough wooden floor.

The ropes were not real tight to begin with and I twisted my wrists one way and the other until they felt looser. The wood rubbed the tender skin on the underside of my wrists and the rope chafed me, until my wrists were abraded almost all the way around. They became slippery with blood soaking in the coarse fibers, lubricating my skin as I tried to ease my hands through the rope loop.

I kept a watchful eye on the demons, but none paid me any attention. They had their backs to me while they watched the duel. From my elevated position, I saw over their heads to the space where Royal fought.

Biting the inside of my mouth, I wriggled my right hand free, wincing as skin on my wrist and back of my hand messily peeled away.

I tried to unpick the rope on my left wrist, but wrenching at it had tightened the knot and I didn't have time to take my time, so to speak. I tore my hand free, removing more skin. I sat up, leaned over, and with shaking hands worked on the ropes around my ankles.

I held my breath as I slowly slid down off the contraption to the ground and stood right behind the demons, afraid one or more would look back at me or hear me move, then backed away from them, but not too far. I looked at the table and saw it sat only a few feet out from the curving wall. I looked around, peering to penetrate the shadowy perimeter of the room, but the single arched opening was the only exit. If I could sneak around the demons, if I could reach the archway, if I could outpace the demons who would surely come after me, if. . . .

I gave up on ifs. I couldn't leave Royal behind.

I hunched over and made my way behind them, back to the table. I was sure they would hear me. With their supersensitive hearing, how could they miss me scrabbling along? But they were totally captivated by the duel. *One step at a time, Tiff.*

When I reached the table, I squatted behind it and rested for a moment. I was so scared I would be seen, that the cries of the demon horde when they saw me would distract Royal, giving the other demon an opportunity to kill him; that Royal would die.

But the longer I waited, the more chance of all that happening. I grabbed the Ruger off the top of my clothes, staggered upright and climbed on the table.

Royal and his dueling partner moved too fast for me to get a bead on them. I spread my legs, lifted the gun in both hands and fired over their heads.

The report sounded like a shot from a cannon, followed by a *ping* as it ricocheted. Most of the demons reflexively ducked. The others froze. Royal and his adversary stopped moving, and stared at me.

As Royal met my eyes across the distance separating us, the demon stepped and spun, his blade making a diagonal at Royal's neck.

I fired again.

I aimed for his shoulder, but my hand shook and the bullet hit him just above the collarbone. The impact spun him halfway around.

Royal took his head off.

The body stayed upright for a instant, then collapsed to the ground. My eyes, and those of every demon, followed the head as it trundled meatily over the wooden boards and hit the wall nose first. It rolled back and came to rest on one cheek.

I dropped to my knees.

Royal raised his head and stared a challenge at the demons. I lifted my gun, expecting all hell to break loose—Royal and I couldn't fight off thirty demons—but they backed away. Convinced they would turn on us, I watched in disbelief as they walked to the wall and passed through the arch in ones and twos. Caesar paused and met my eyes, but I couldn't read his expression, then he followed the rest of them.

Royal lowered his bloody sword, then dropped it. It hit the boards with a clatter. I didn't see him move. He was just here, arms reaching for me, easing me off the table. He went to his knees, taking me with him, gently holding me, my face in his chest, my legs sprawled on the floor. I couldn't take my finger out of the trigger guard of my Ruger and my hand clenched the butt so hard it was bloodless.

"Tiff," he said softly in my hair. "Can you stand? We have to get out of here."

I wanted to stay on his knees. I didn't want him to ever let me go. But I nodded on his chest. He eased me off his knees, stood, and helped me upright. Reaction set in, and I shook, the Ruger jerking in my grasp. I let him take it out my hand, then his arms enfolded me again. I felt hard metal on my naked spine and his fingers move to engage the safety.

"Ow!" I said.

He pushed me to arm's length, brows almost meeting just above his nose as his gaze swept my body. "You're hurt."

And naked. And Royal Mortensen is seeing all of me, I thought, as if it mattered under the circumstances.

He let me go, undid the top two buttons of his shirt, lost patience and ripped it open. Buttons popped off and flew everywhere. Bunching the material, he used the shirt to gently wipe drying blood from my body. The little nicks were not deep and the bleeding had already stopped. He tore the material in strips with appalling ease and bound my wrists. He looked me over again, and apparently satisfied, helped me dress and put my necklace, bracelet, watch and the Ruger in my pockets.

With his arm along my shoulders, we crossed the room to get his jacket.

He bent to pluck it from the floor and tried to drape it over me.

"Are we going home?"

"If we are lucky."

I can be practical at the strangest times. "Then you'd better wear it, else you'll be a mite conspicuous in Clarion. What do you mean, *if we're lucky*?"

He put his arm around my waist and turned me in the other direction. "We have an hour to get out of here. It's a big place."

"Why an hour?"

"The tradition of combat dictates the victor has one hour to quit a hostile arena." He frowned at me. "But surely you knew."

"Knew what?"

"The rules of challenge. That we would go free if I won the duel."

"How in *hell* could I possibly know that?" I said as I shook my head.

He grasped me by the shoulder and held me in place. "But. . . . What did you think you were doing?" He looked aghast. "You did not *think*, did you. You and your little gun—"

"I *did* think! Kind of. I figured if I shot enough of them we could make a break for it." I wrenched my shoulder free. "And it's not a little gun."

I didn't understand what he said beneath his breath, but I'm sure it wasn't complimentary. He put his hand in the small of my back and propelled me onward.

His feet slowed, stopped, and I saw we stood between the body and the head near the wall. Royal just stood there, looking at the head with an odd, angry . . . yearning.

"Who is he?" I asked in a low voice.

Royal glanced at the body with emptiness in his eyes. "My brother Kien."

What do you say to a man who just killed his own brother? What could you say? Nothing would be adequate. I looked at Kien's head and felt no remorse or horror that an evil man lost his life, but I felt terrible Royal had to be the one who did it.

As if he read my thoughts, he put one finger under my chin and tilted my head up. "It would have happened eventually. It was inevitable," he said stiffly. "He was always corrupt, even as a child. Although this is the first time we fought one-on-one, it is not the first time he tried to kill me. We were of the same blood, but never true kin."

There must be *something* I should say, but I couldn't think what. I stuttered out something unintelligible.

"It would be better if we do not discuss it farther." Royal smiled thinly. "Change the subject, you are good at that."

In other circumstances, I would take umbrage at the remark, but I swallowed and obeyed.

We walked to the arched opening and the set of stone steps going up. They rose steeply; the bluish illumination came from brighter blue light at the top. I looked back. "What is this place?"

"It is Morté Tescién, my ancestral home." He took my hand and led me up the steps.

I watched where I put my feet. "When you say home, do you mean like in *house*?"

"Yes, Tiff."

"So what's down there, the basement?"

"Part of it. An area not in use at the moment."

Good grief! "Just how big *is* this place?"

"Think White House."

Two more steps, and it clicked. His brother called him Ryel. Morté Tescién. Ryel Morté Tescién. Royal Mortensen. "You changed your name."

"No. I'm Royal Eric Mortensen, born and raised in Eau Claire, Wisconsin. But I was also born Ryel, of House Morté Tescién."

A square passage stretched away from the top of the steps. The size, wide as it was high, with floor, walls and ceiling lined in glossy, glowing cobalt-blue tiles, gave it a crazy three-dimensional effect. It seemed to go on forever; I couldn't see where it ended. Royal's fingers twined with mine and we walked on.

The first right angle came upon us suddenly. I might have walked into the facing wall if not for his hand guiding me. The floor gradually sloped until I felt the pressure of walking uphill in my calves and ankles.

"We are in the maintenance levels," he said. "Everything required for the smooth running of the House is tucked away down here. It feels empty. I think they are distancing themselves from what happened below."

Another staircase, another passageway with silvery, polished metal doors, some open, others closed. I glimpsed small square rooms lined with metal shelves on which square and rectangular cartons sat in stacks, objects wrapped in murky plastic, tin cans. Furniture with missing legs, or arms, or chipped woodwork filled another room. We passed what were obviously clerical offices.

"Whoa!" I said in a low voice when we were safely past. "Computers? Phones?"

Royal gave me a *so?* look.

I brought my brows together. "But your . . . those guys downstairs . . . the clothes and swords . . . I thought you were, well, medieval."

Alert, he kept his eyes ahead. "It's an affectation, Tiff. We are a modern society."

"Oh. Is demon technology like ours, then? Do you have all the good junk; cell phones and Blue Ray and electronic games?" I thought of an appliance I consider indispensable. "And microwave ovens; do you have microwaves?"

"Demon? You call us demons?"

Uh oh. I watched my feet pace the smooth ceramic tiles. "Well, it's the pointy teeth and glittering eyes, you see."

I kept my head down, but rolled my eyes up to see his face. I expected I had at least irritated him, at most insulted him, but he tilted his chin up and let out a laugh. Grinning, he met my eyes. "Then it's as well I don't have pointed teeth."

"I'm sorry."

"No, it's okay." He shook his head. "Men with pointed teeth can be nothing else but demons." And he chortled again.

"They're only a tiny bit pointed," I said defensively. "It's not like your guys have fangs."

Another rising stair, then we passed three arched openings which looked in on one enormous kitchen. The appliances looked state of the art, and they filled the perimeter of the room. Next came two big pantries, a room stuffed with huge freezers, another room equipped with washing machines, tumble dryers and sinks.

We took a left to a blank-walled passage. A question came into my mind. "How did you know where to find me?"

His fingers tightened on mine. "A hunch, or call it deductive reasoning. You called Mike, and the line went dead before he could say a word. We looked for you. I found your phone on the ground near the apartment block, but I took it before Mike saw. We split up and I went to your house. Your car was still outside. It looked bad."

He looked at me. "I believe in you, Tiff. I read up on your cases. You're the real thing, you are no quack. You said Charlie Geary identified me, but I did not kill him. I knew you would not accuse me out of spite."

"You did, did you?"

His smile was gentle. "You are a stubborn, hot-headed, argumentative woman, but you are a *good* woman. You would not falsely accuse an innocent man. You and Charlie gave me the identity of the killer."

"And you thought maybe he took me?"

His smile dropped away. "Thank the Lady I was right."

"Guess I should be glad Mike didn't stow you in lockup and throw away the key."

"He returned my gun and badge when we got back to the precinct."

Although I was joking about Mike putting him in a cell, the truth was a letdown. I mean, I didn't want Royal arrested and thrown in jail and I didn't reckon Mike would go that far anyway, maybe put him on paid leave, but he waited till I left the PD and acted like nothing happened in Granby! "I wasn't sure he believed me, but I thought he would at least go through the formalities."

My feelings must have been apparent. "Be realistic, Tiff. Your word against mine? Did you really think he would lock me up while he looked for proof?"

"Yes. No. But he one-hundred-percent ignored what I told him. If he did that with every case I worked for him, there'd—"

"Mike is a clever and intuitive man. Perhaps he has a little latent psychic ability himself. He gets a feeling about the people you give him. He did not get the same feeling about me."

He could be right. Perhaps Mike's intuition told him to listen to me the second time I marched in his office and said he had to. He threw me out the first time. I went back six months later and gave him information I shouldn't know on a murder victim, and this time he heard me out. My input placed a murderer behind bars, but still, it was a leap of faith on Mike's part if ever there was one.

I was so tired, and all those glowing blue tiles made my head ache, and Royal walked so fast. I tried to keep up so he didn't have to haul me along, but as we took another turn and he led me to yet another stairwell, I stumbled.

Before I knew what was happening, he bent, put one arm around my back, the other beneath my knees, and whisked me up in his arms.

I let out a tiny, surprised shriek. I had never been gathered up and held to a man's chest before. I flung my arms around his neck and held on tight, my cheek on his silken hair. He strode up the steps with me tightly hugged to him. Being held closely and carefully felt really nice, so I decided not to object. After a minute I let go one of my hands and laid my palm on his chest, on skin as smooth and silken as his hair. I thought I'd stay there for a while. Maybe a week or two.

Royal paced the floor with a stride so smooth we seemed to float. "Don't be frightened, Tiff. I won't let anything happen to you."

Not the reason my fingers couldn't stop exploring his chest.

He went on, his tone deepening, "You shouldn't be here. I should have protected you."

"Not your fault."

"It was my fault. I knew the danger you were in; I should have been with you. I will not leave your side again, Tiff."

Aw, I thought, then rethought. My voice rose. "Now just one minute—"

He touched my lips with his index finger. "Not so loud," he cautioned.

Okay, I would save it till later, because if he meant that literally and thought he could be with me every minute of the day, voices *would* be raised. I didn't need a watchdog.

We were in a high-ceilinged passage, the ceiling a deep blood-red, the walls covered in red flocked wallpaper, the floor carpeted in a flowing red and black design. "Why do we have to be quiet? I thought they couldn't touch us for an hour."

He spoke softly in my ear. "Our hour is almost up. We must take care now. If they know where we are, they will converge, hoping our time runs out."

Anxiety crawled a slimy trail through my gut. I couldn't go back to that basement.

When we stepped inside a large room, it looked as if the demons had already converged. An impression of high ceilings, huge windows letting in swathes of sunlight, the sparkle of gilt and crystal, space and airiness, railed galleries up high, but mostly I saw demons, watching us with glimmering eyes. Some of them wore tights and tunics and I recognized the demons from the cavern below among them. Others wore modern clothing you see on Americans walking the streets of Clarion. All were male, and I wondered if they kept their women hidden away, or if the room was strictly a male domain.

"Put me down," I said in Royal's ear. I wanted my feet on the ground and control over my movements.

He took no notice, and I did not dare make a scene.

I saw Caesar at the back of the room, looking at me with hard sapphire eyes. I couldn't suppress a shudder. Royal's arms tightened on me.

"Hold on, Tiff," he said.

We didn't go at full demon speed, but we definitely *moved*. The room became a whirl of glass, flesh and metal, jewel tone colors and glittering eyes. I closed my eyes, unable to cope with a feeling of disorientation and the beginnings of nausea. Thankfully, we slowed and came to a stop before I destroyed the romance of being passionately held to a man's naked chest by throwing up all over him.

We were in another passageway. He set me down. I clung to him as I looked ahead. I saw nothing but blank stone walls and a dark arch.

I looked back. Demons crowded the passage. Motionless, expressionless, they watched us.

And he opened up his wings and flew us out of there.

Just kidding.

We stepped through a door, and I didn't realize how hard my nails dug in Royal's back till they started to hurt. He lowered me to my feet.

Clarion's Montague Square surrounded us now. No trace of the Otherworld. I got free of his arm and turned to look back at a plain wood door in an otherwise blank brick wall. I couldn't recall seeing it before.

Two women toting shopping bags walked up from behind us. They passed, and both looked back at Royal over their shoulders. Eyeing me, he buttoned up his jacket.

I checked my watch. Seven-fifteen. Two and a half hours, to be abducted, tortured, and watch Royal cut off his brother's head. Oh, and I mustn't forget that included just short of an hour getting out of Morté Tescién.

Royal gently turned me in the other direction. "Hold onto me. We're going to Clarion Regional."

"With what are obviously rope burns and abrasions? I don't think so. I'll doctor it at home."

His mouth set stubbornly. I started walking.

"Tiff, where are we going?" he asked at my back.

"To find Lawrence."

Chapter Eighteen

———♈———

A half-hour later and Gorge's Antique Emporium would have been locked up for the night. We walked in to find Gorge amid antique furniture and display cabinets, chatting to two customers as he wrote them a receipt. He glanced up, smiled, looked back at his customers; then the tan leached from his face as his brain registered exactly who came in his shop.

So demons blanched. I was gathering *so* much information for Lynn.

Paler with each passing second, he chatted with his clients in a stilted way as he walked them to the door. He shut it, flipped the sign and pulled down the blind to let prospective customers know he had closed the shop.

He turned to us and clasped his hands at his waist as he looked at Royal. I don't think he even noticed me. He dropped his hands to his sides and bowed over, held the pose a few seconds, and straightened up. "My Lord?"

My Lord?

Royal got right to the point. "Do you know the whereabouts of Lawrence Marchant?"

"Lawrence Marchant?" Gorge asked, not at all convincingly.

I took the paper from my pocket, unfolded it and held it up. "I found receipts and evaluations for furniture you sold to Lindy. And you were their friend. Lawrence even drew a picture of you."

I held my breath. Gorge continued to stare. He stiffened when Royal walked up to him, and clenched his fists, arms straight at his sides. I tensed. Would he attack Royal? If I ignored his alien features, he looked like a prosperous merchant in his dark-green three-piece suit and leather wing-tipped brogues, but he was a demon, and perhaps a match for Royal in speed and strength.

Royal stopped several paces from Gorge and very slowly swiveled to turn his back on the shorter demon. With one hand, he lifted his long copper-gold hair away from the nape of his neck to reveal a tiny tattoo of a golden creature bordered with black right on his hairline.

Gorge's shoulders sagged and he relaxed. "Thank the Lady!"

Just who was this Lady everyone liked to thank?

Royal shook his hair back, covering the tat. Gorge gestured to the back of the shop. "This way, my Lord. I kept the boy safe, praying someone from your House would find us."

"Does he know?" Royal asked Gorge.

"That everything in his life has changed?" George nodded confirmation.

I was definitely out of the loop—what the hell just happened? Who was the Lady and was a House more than only a big old home? If I were not mistaken, both had capital letters. Royal turned back to me and I looked askance, but he ignored my expression. He looked different, as if he had gained height, and he held himself stiffly erect. He looked . . . well . . . he looked *lordly*, if there is such a word. Regal, maybe?

Regal Royal? I mused as Gorge went to the back of the shop, wending through the clutter to where a long burgundy velvet curtain hung on the wall. He pulled the curtain aside to reveal a wooden door, opened it on a staircase and gestured us through.

But Royal put his hands on my shoulders, effectively keeping me in place. "I think you should wait here. I do not know how Lawrence will react and the fewer converging on him the better."

A little boy who saw his mother die, whisked away from everything and everyone he knew. Now complete strangers were poised to tell him something extraordinary. I could see the sense in what Royal said. "Okay."

Royal gestured for Gorge to lead the way and followed him up the steps.

I sank on a convenient brocade-padded bench and listened to the tick of Gorge's clocks. I like the soft *tock* of the mantle clock in my bedroom, it lulls me, but listening to the dozen or more in the shop all day long would get on my nerves. I would be gritting my teeth in no time at all. I almost fell off the bench when every one of them chimed the hour.

I looked at the thick curtain, wondering what happened in Gorge's apartment, and marveled I trusted two demons with the safety of a little boy. I had an issue with trust, one amongst many. I counted on someone once but it ended badly, and since then had distanced myself so I couldn't make the same mistake. Yet I trusted Royal, I knew that by the staggering relief I experienced when he appeared in Morté Tescién, though he turned out to be Kien in disguise. I knew it when Royal carried me out of the cavern. Having faith in another person was something of a novelty.

When did my perception change? When did I see him as a man, not an alien creature with evil intentions; as an honest cop, not a creature posing as one? As someone on whom I could rely?

I couldn't pinpoint the moment. Perhaps it was as far back as the first night in my bedroom, when he cupped my face in gentle hands and kissed me.

I waited.

Royal came down the stairs so silently I didn't notice him till he spoke. He sat beside me on the bench.

"Is everything okay?"

"More or less. He understands what's happened, and what is to come."

I sagged tiredly. "I don't, Royal. Was Gorge at Lindy's apartment when she died? What has he to do with all this? Is Lawrence really safe now?"

Several heartbeats of silence, followed by, "You were right: Gorge and Lindy were friends. He went to see her the day she died. He heard her cry out and found her in the bathroom. She was dying, Tiff. Gorge tried to bring her back by forcing some of his energy into her, but it did not work."

"You can . . . what do you mean, put his energy in her?"

"A tiny bit of psychic energy." He smiled a small sad smile. "It's a demon thing. If you look closely at Gorge you will see lines on his face which were not there a week ago."

I didn't ask for a scientific explanation—I see dead people; I don't need justification for every mystical ability or event.

"You know I can sense other Gelpha, it's an innate ability all of us possess. Gorge—"

"You're called Gelpha?" I said, feeling dumb. *Of course they have a name, and it's not* demon.

"Yes. And although you haven't asked, our world is Bel-Athaer. You will find mention of it in your ancient lore."

"I don't recall the name."

He gave me an amused smile. "Have you never heard of the Land Beneath the Waves?"

I gawped at him. "You're elves?"

He hiccupped out a laugh. "You confuse Celtic lore with fairy tales. Ancient Druids knew of The Land Beneath the Waves, or the Otherworld. The *waves* they spoke of were aetheric, an alternate plane coexisting with theirs."

He didn't give me time to think that over. "Although we had not met, Gorge knew I was in Clarion, but not the position I hold. If he had, he would have come to me. He brought Lawrence here, then sensed Caesar and his partner Phaid. He went back to Lindy's apartment and cleared out all traces of Lawrence and brought away photos of his mother, so the boy could have them. He waited till night and went to every tenant, and made them forget Lawrence." He met my eyes. "I know that must gall you, but it was necessary." His gaze drifted away. "Not knowing what else to do, Gorge planned to take Lawrence to Berne, Switzerland, where he has another shop. Lawrence would pose as his son."

"But why? Why not take Lawrence to the authorities? Why were they after the boy? Why did they kill all those children?"

"I think you will understand when you meet Lawrence." He stood and presented his hand to me.

I stayed put. "Wait a minute. You said you've looked for the killers for years—you just mentioned a position of some kind."

"I'm an enforcer for the ruling House." His hand went to the nape of his neck. "The tattoo identifies me as such. Rules govern those of us who live among you and my job is to ensure they are adhered to." His eyes went steely. "I failed miserable with the children." Then he took my hand and hauled me upright.

"And you gotta explain this House thing," I said as he led me to the curtain. He held it aside and preceded me up the steps.

At the top of the staircase, we emerged in Gorge's apartment, into a small square hall with doors front and to the sides. A small Oriental rug lay on the floor and a large, tasteful but nonetheless artificial plant in a brown ceramic pot sat on the floor beside the facing door. Gorge waited in the open doorway.

I followed him into the living room, but I barely notice the décor. I was transfixed by the sight of a small, beautiful brown-haired boy sitting on a chaise lounge, his bright eyes lighting up at sight of Gorge.

A little boy with sparkling eyes and pointed teeth.

His gaze switched to me, and his smile widened. In something of a daze, I went over and knelt at his feet, looking up at him. His smile wavered as I continued to stare.

I couldn't come up with anything cheerful or reassuring to say to a child who just lost his mother. *He's just a little boy*, I told myself, yet something old looked out of his eyes.

I cleared my throat. "Lawrence, do you understand what happened to your mom?"

"Yes. She died, so Gorge is looking after me," he said in a high, sweet voice. He looked to where Gorge and Royal stood. Gorge gave him an encouraging nod. "We're going to live in Bel-Athaer, with my family."

"No no no," Gorge chastised gently. "*You* are going to Bel-Athaer. You'll love it."

Lawrence's little shoulders straightened. He said, his tone cool, "Gorge is coming with me."

Gorge wrung his hands together. "I'm gratified by the honor, Lord Lawrence, but my business won't run itself," he said rather condescendingly.

"But I want you to come."

"I am sorry, but it's not possible. Perhaps—"

"You *will* come," Lawrence said in a deeper tone as his eyes darkened.

Startled, I went back on my heels, with the conviction Lawrence was no helpless child. Gorge called him Lord—he was an important person in the land of Bel-Athaer. I recalled Father Robert's words, about Lawrence's following at school, how the other kids seemed drawn to him. A Lord, who already had a Court of willing little human children; who was already accustomed to being obeyed.

Gorge knew it too. Looking panicked, he fluttered his fingers in the air. "But my Lord, I am banished!"

"I've decided you're not," Lawrence said.

Gorge went to a glass-fronted bookcase. He chose a large, heavy book and showed me the spine as he went back to the bedroom. "He wants a bedtime story," he said with a roll of his eyes. *The Tales of the Brothers Grimm.*

I stood with my back to the window overlooking Eccles Avenue, arms folded over my chest. Royal faced me from the other side of the room. I think my expression said I'd had enough of mystery and vague words. I wanted answers.

He went to a chaise lounge upholstered in pale-blue silk. "Come here, Tiff. Please."

I joined him. We sat side by side. I heard the low, rhythmic burr of Gorge's voice from the bedroom, then he fell silent. Gorge crept into the living room and eased the bedroom door closed. "Fast asleep. The poor mite is exhausted."

"Is that any way to address your master?" Royal said.

Gorge's mouth popped open, then he realized Royal teased him and flapped an admonishing hand.

"So you were banished from Bel-Athaer?" I asked him.

"Royal's father exiled me for a *teensy* misdemeanor."

Royal snorted.

Gorge glared at him. "A *misdemeanor*," he insisted. He crossed one leg over the other and laid his wrist on his knee. "Anyway, I prefer life here." His expression twisted and he slumped. "I like it here," he said plaintively.

"It will not be so bad," Royal said. "Think of all the attention you will receive at court as the High Lord's favorite."

High Lord? That definitely sounded important.

"That's what I'm afraid of. I remember life at court all too well," said Gorge disconsolately.

I sprang to my feet. "Okay! Enough! You two tell me *everything*, from the beginning."

"I'm not saying a word," from Gorge.

"You will be more comfortable here," Royal said, patting the chaise lounge. "Please."

So I sat again, rather heavily. Gorge winced as my backside hit the piece of antique furniture.

"I need to go back in time to explain what happened," Royal began. "The High Lady was assassinated fifty years ago, and—"

"High Lady?"

"Think Queen," Gorge mouthed.

"Explain please," I said tersely.

Royal's hand came down on mine and the warmth of his skin, well, it made me feel somewhat better. "The peoples of Bel-Athaer belong to what we call Houses, which I suppose are comparable to small nations. There are between five and six hundred at present. Each of these domains is overseen by a ruling Lord or Lady and they in turn answer to the High Lord, or High Lady. The titles are hereditary."

"Like in medieval Europe?"

"Hereditary inheritance is a tradition still followed by countries in your world."

"It's when some power-hungry asshole way back when decided he had a god-given right to rule, and wanted to keep it in the family."

He grinned. "Whatever. Whoever we are, we cling to tradition." His smile blinked out. "The High Lady was assassinated fifty years ago and since then we have warred among ourselves. Without her ruling hand, Bel-Athaer dissolved into chaos. Lacking a High ruler, House fought House for land, for power, for wealth. Many Houses were overcome and amalgamated with the victor's. Fifty years, Tiff. Fifty years of war."

His eyes took on a faraway look. I wondered if he fought in those wars, if he killed, if he lost family or friends.

He continued: "We clung to one hope: the Heir would return. When the High Lady died, we learned of a plot to kill him and his family, so we brought them here. They went underground, so deep underground they went off our radar. Lawrence is the heir's grandson, ruler by right of blood and power, the High Lord."

I tried to absorb that. Little Lawrence, a child, was supposed to rule an entire warmongering race? It didn't seem possible.

"Lawrence will assume his position. He will be trained and advised. When he gains his full power, he will bend every Lord and Lady in Bel-Athaer to his will. He will bring peace."

I looked at Gorge. "You weren't just Lindy's friend, were you."

He dropped his chin, looking at his hands. "I knew about Lawrence the first time he and Lindy came in the Emporium. But Bel-Athaer is forbidden me, I couldn't go back, or contact the High House. So I kept my eye on them. I knew someone would eventually come after Lawrence. I hoped his House would find him, but I knew others would be searching."

"To kill him."

Gorge nodded glumly.

"Not only did I fail the High House, my family were traitors," Royal said. "They murdered hundreds of innocent half-human, half-Gelpha children because one of them could, possibly, be the new Heir."

"His Lordship does not blame you for what your brother did," Gorge said.

"He knows?" I asked.

"He knows," Gorge confirmed.

"Did Lindy know, about Lawrence's father?"

Royal shook his head as he answered me. "One of her forebears had Gelpha blood in his veins. It was weak in her, but allowed her to carry the High Lord's bloodline."

I stiffened my spine and eyed him narrowly. "So what was she, a broodmare?"

"Lindy called him a one-night-stand and said he captivated her the moment she saw him. She couldn't resist him," Gorge said, looking abashed.

I knew what he implied. Lawrence's father used his power on Lindy. She thought she loved him, maybe she did, but not of her own free will.

Gorge saw my downturned mouth. "I'm sorry, Miss Banks. He must have had his reasons. We don't know what happened to his father and mother, why he didn't come out of hiding, or return to Bel-Athaer. For motives unknown to us, he sired a child and disappeared again. He couldn't stay with Lindy and risk leading his enemies to his son. And Lindy loved Lawrence with all her heart. She didn't regret . . . anything."

He didn't know that. I imagined Lindy pining for a man who would never return, looking at her son and seeing the father's face. Then I had a thought. "How did your people know about Lawrence?"

I thought I saw reluctance on Royal's face, followed by resignation. "Every House has a Seer," he said, again using capital letters. "Every one of them shared the same vision six years ago. On November 9th, 2002, somewhere in your world, an heir was born."

"Seer as in wise man," I scoffed. "And you call yourself a modern society?"

"Take care how you speak of them, Tiff," Gorge said in an almost-whisper. "They are very powerful."

"I hardly think they'll hear me. So these Seers predicted the birth, and every House knew about it."

"They sent their people to find him, some to welcome him home, others to kill him," Royal said, absolutely *not* amused.

"They abducted the boys or killed them outright," said Gorge.

"Like Charlie Geary," I said sadly. "So they are dead, all of them."

Royal leaned on my shoulder. "All part-Gelpha male children. Once they saw the assassins, they couldn't be allowed to live to identify their killers."

Chapter Nineteen

─────♈─────

I woke stretched out on the chaise lounge, my head on Royal's knees, his palm resting lightly on my hair. Someone had removed my shoes, which sat together on the carpet. Evidently, I fell asleep in the middle of a conversation with Gorge and Royal. It felt like early morning. I looked at an ornate black and gold onyx clock on a low cabinet. Six-thirty.

Lawrence bounced into the room. "I'm going to stab someone with a sword!"

"Only if necessary, Lord Lawrence," said Gorge, following on the boy's heels. "There will also be studying and homework."

Lawrence scowled, looking like an ordinary little boy when told he has to do extra school work, except he sparkled. Then he charged back to the bedroom, slashing the air with an imaginary sword.

"You told him he will stab people?" Royal asked Gorge.

"Certainly not! I was talking about his lessons and when I mentioned weaponry and the martial arts, he asked what I meant."

I roused myself. Royal helped me upright. "Hello, Tiff," he said softly.

"Hello, you," I replied with a soppy smile. "Will Lawrence really get to learn how to use a sword? He's six!"

"He'll learn to use every weapon known to your world and mine. The sword is traditional."

"And traditionally used in duels?" I asked, recalling the flash of polished metal as Royal fought his brother in the depths of Morté Tescién. "You guys are big on tradition in the nastiest ways."

"Tradition has a depth of meaning only those who were slaves can understand," Gorge said.

I intercepted a look between them. Royal was not happy Gorge brought that up. Gorge cringed.

We have committed many acts of atrocity, we who call ourselves human beings, as if the title makes us humane, although I never heard or read of the enslavement of people like Royal's. "But we're weaklings compared to you guys. How could we—?"

Royal cut me off. "You were not our masters." I thought I saw loathing in his eyes. He sounded . . . upset, and angry, and . . . uneasy. He looked at his clasped hands. "We don't speak of them. It was a long time ago, Tiff. Don't ask."

I saw the enormous conceit of my assumption, so I didn't ask. Which didn't mean I would not one day; but not now.

"We should be going," Royal said.

I smiled at Gorge. "What about you, Gorge? Are you leaving soon?"

"Right after you." He sighed heavily as he looked around his living room. "Someone will take care of the Emporium for me. Me, I'm off to Bel-Athaer and a life of . . . tagging along behind the High Lord I suppose."

Poor Gorge, who thought he did his good deed and could go back to posing as an incredibly cute but rather twee young man.

Lawrence emerged from the bedroom, went to Gorge and took his hand. He looked up at Gorge's face. "I need you, Gorge."

Gorge forced a bright smile. "Which makes everything all right, then, doesn't it!"

"Good-bye, Lawrence," I said. I couldn't bring myself to call him Lord.

The boy eyed me solemnly. "Good-bye Miss Banks. Thank you."

I felt Royal's hand on my shoulder. "Come on. I brought the truck over while you slept."

As we went downstairs, I heard Lawrence. "Gorge, where are my pictures of momma?"

"In your backpack."

"Where's my backpack?"

"I don't know," Gorge said rather snappishly. "Where did you leave it, young Law . . . my Lord?"

Royal held the wheel in a tight-knuckled grip, driving with grim determination. I tried to break the heavy silence and succeeded in putting my big ol' foot in my big ol' mouth. "You mentioned your family."

"I meant my people, my clan. My mother and father died in the wars. My brother was Lord of Morté Tescién."

His fingers dug in the leather-covered steering wheel. "The High House will avenge the murders and the attempted assassination of the High Lord."

I had already thought of that. "I'm sorry your House was responsible."

"Morté Tescién is no longer my House. I was sixteen when my uncle and his family were murdered and my father returned to Bel-Athaer as Lord of Morté Tescién. I transferred my allegiance to the High House when called to serve as an enforcer."

"You can change Houses?"

"Only if you go to the High House. Otherwise, you remain with the House to which you are born."

I decided to keep my mouth shut; now was not the time to bug him with a heap of questions. He must be as exhausted as I felt, and I felt awful despite a sleep so heavy I didn't know he left to get his truck. I wondered if he dwelled on the events of the past hours, how he killed his brother to save my life. No matter what he said about their relationship, they were brothers and that had to mean something.

I wouldn't know. If I my family were still alive, they were a mystery to me.

I thought about Lindy Marchant. I hoped she went to where she should be and did not haphazardly wander around Clarion. I like to think it's a happy place. I guess I'll find out when I get there.

I thought about Lawrence's father making Lindy want him, love him, and Caesar's partner Phaid putting his will on me. Royal didn't do that to me and never tried, but had he ever used the faculty to influence a human being?

Demons could *control* the mind and heart of the unwary; that opened up horrific possibilities. A demon in a position of power could do untold damage to our society.

I thought about Lawrence Marchant, an eerie amalgamation of little human boy and alien Lord.

We left downtown Clarion and drove through The Avenues, street after street of Victorian mansions, most of them converted to apartments. The majority look sad, the paint on window- and door frames chipped, their cookie-cutter moldings dirty and faded. Landlords buy them cheap and don't want to put more money than necessary to their upkeep. The wealthy elite once lived here, but now it belongs to the downtrodden. I often walk The Avenues because the trees are so big they cast shade full across the streets, and no one bothers me. People up here mind their own business.

I noticed Royal kept checking his rear- and side-view mirrors and nausea churned in my stomach. I twisted in my seat to look back at the street falling behind us, hoping to not see a following automobile. "Will they come after us?"

"I'm watching for the boys in blue. Mike put an APB out on you."

Oh. Shit.

A cryptic few words, the line goes dead, I'm nowhere to be found—of course Mike suspected the worse. "Have you still got my cell?"

He dipped in his pocket and handed me my phone. I turned it on. Five incoming calls from Clarion PD. I would find some on my home phone too.

We climbed Beeches Street. I hiked my body up, waiting to see the roof of my house. In the cavern, I thought I would never see my house again, and knew how much it meant to me. My home was the one stable thing in my life. Oh, yeah, along with my permanent fixtures, Jack and Mel.

Royal parked his truck in the street and we got out. The sun hung just above the mountains behind the house, but snow cloaked the peaks and mottled the slopes below. Frost dusted what was left of my plants in their bed beneath the kitchen window. Time to hang my down coat on the rack in the hall, put my boots in the tray beneath.

Except I didn't have a coat-rack and tray anymore.

It felt good to put my feet on the path to my house, good to fit my key in the lock and push the door open.

Mac sat in the hall. He looked up at Royal. "Bad boy!" Royal said sternly. "Bad boy, Mac!"

I went to my knees. "You can't call him bad when he hasn't done anything."

"He wants to. I can see it in his eyes."

I reached for Mac, and he slit his eyes, stepped back, presented his rear and trundled to the kitchen.

I got myself upright and went after him, Royal right behind me. Mac stood over his empty bowl, looking in it as if he thought food would miraculous rise up and fill the thing.

"Well. Look who's here, *Tiffany* and the Iron Chef," came Jack's mocking voice.

"Finally decided to come home, did you?" said Mel. "I suppose fun with Mister Hunky blew any thought of us right out your mind."

I ignored them; I had to with Royal in the room. I went to the pantry and got Mac's kibble. He dipped his nose in the bowl before I finished filling it and I swear he *inhaled* the tiny nuggets.

Royal sniffed the air. "Can you smell something?"

"Yeah. See it too." I eyed the puddle by the backdoor and the malodorous brown pile next to it.

"Disgusting little beast," Jack sneered.

I got some old newspaper from the recycle bin under the sink, a bottle of pine disinfectant, a rag, paper towel, and went to the door, trying not to breathe through my nose. I spoke to Royal, but not for his benefit alone. "Not his fault. I wasn't here to let him out."

After dealing with Mac's thoughtful gift and putting it in the bin out back, I sank in a kitchen chair and rubbed my brow with the back of my hand. "I don't know why I'm so worn out. I slept heavy."

"But not long enough," Royal said as he took the chair opposite me.

"You found time to sleep?" Mel said.

Jack chimed in. "Bet she needed it after all the exercise."

"Why don't you get some sleep," Royal said.

"Sounds good, but I need a shower."

He gave me an intense look, a little something smoldering in his eyes. "I could do with one of those."

I'm sure I went bright red. He gave me a toothy grin.

"And then I better go see Mike."

He grunted, expression suddenly sober. "What will you tell him?"

"I'll think of something," I said unhappily. "What about you?"

He shrugged. "I gave up looking for you and went off duty."

"You better report in before he gets suspicious."

His mouth crooked. "I guess a shower will have to wait."

But neither of us moved.

Then he pushed to his feet and came to me. I stood to meet him. When his arms came around my waist I clung to him. He ran his hand down my arm, brushing one of the tiny nicks on my shoulder. I sucked air through my teeth. He jerked back from me. "I'm sorry, I forgot."

And I forgot my vow to not speak His name in vain. *Je-sus Christ!* "Oh poo!" I said elegantly. "I'm a tough girl. Now come here."

"And you need rest."

The man had *way* too much self-control. "Royal," I whispered, "if you don't kiss me right now, I'll make you wish you never came to Clarion."

If you wanted to see a visible definition of a demonic grin, Royal had it down pat. "We can't have that," he said hoarsely.

His mouth nibbled up my neck to my ear and I savored every touch of lips and teeth, until we were face to face, our lips a hair's breadth apart. I wanted to feel his mouth on mine with desperation I had never known before, not with any man. Mike be damned. He could wait.

The phone rang. We ignored it. I no longer heard the insistent trill as Royal's lips caressed mine.

It was everything I remembered, everything I could imagine, more than a kiss. Delectable warmth stole through me, eradicating my tension. My entire body relaxed. I felt loose and tingly, as if I would turn liquid and melt into a puddle.

Maybe a century later, my lips had been so thoroughly worked over, they burned, and I was having a little problem with breathing. He put his hands to my head and ran his fingers back through my hair, moved them to cup my face and looked in my eyes with intensity powerful enough to melt stone. I eased back a few inches as he pushed my shirt off one shoulder, allowing him access to my collarbone; a gentle nibble there, and his lips moved to my earlobe. Drowning in his touch, I closed my eyes and let my head fall back.

"Tiff, if you're there pick up the goddamn phone!" Mike said.

The Lieutenant's voice went through my head like a saw-tooth blade, effectively destroying the mood. As Royal lifted his head and looked past me at the phone, I silently cursed Mike to hell and back.

"I can disconnect the phone," I whispered, as if Mike could hear me.

Royal smiled in a pained way. "He's furious. He'll get worse the longer you leave it."

I wrinkled my nose. "Yeah, you're right."

Royal took his arms from around me as if doing so were a major effort. I felt cold without his warmth cloaking me. I went to the counter and picked up the phone. "Hello, Mike. I suppose—"

He cut me off, but at least his voice gentled. "Are you all right?"

"I'm fine. Now, I know you—"

"You're fine. Nothing wrong? Nothing at all?"

"Yeah, really, Mike. I was—"

His voice erupted in my ear, making me wince. "In my office! Now!"

I made a face at Royal. Feeling contrary, I told Mike, "I can be there in an hour or two."

"Wilson is two blocks away, he can swing over, pick you up."

"No!" I looked at Royal with alarm. That's all we needed: Officer Ken Wilson seeing Royal's truck parked outside. "No need to pull Ken off his beat. I'll be there in ten. Okay?"

"You do that."

I replaced the phone and let my shoulders sag. "I better get it over with."

"I'll see you later," Royal said.

"Royal," I said as he neared the door, "those tights . . . you ever wear them?"

He paused in the doorway, swung to face me. A slow smile stretched his mouth. "Not as a habit. Would you like me to?"

Supporting myself with a hand on the back of a kitchen chair, I dipped my head as I nonchalantly swung one foot back and forth, "Well not, you know, where anyone else can see you."

"But where you can see me?"

I managed a casual shrug.

"I'm sure I can. . . ," he began slowly, followed by a pause, then, "Are you *teasing* me?"

I looked up to see his face alight with a delighted grin. "I learned from a pro," I said, smirking.

His shook his head, his smile now tender. "You're quite a woman. Do you know that?"

I didn't know what brought that on, so I shrugged again.

He seemed to gather himself together. "I should be going, and so should you. Later, Tiff."

"You can bet on it," I replied huskily.

His gaze lingered on my lips, then he smiled wryly. "Keep those rope burns covered when you shower."

"*Rope burns!*" Mel all but shrieked.

I'm proud I didn't flinch, because I totally forgot my roommates were here. That never happened before. Mind you, they were untypically quiet while Royal and I were absorbed in each other. I could only stare at them, trying to emit displeasure without changing my expression.

Jack chortled, and you don't know how peculiar it is to hear a person laugh when their expression does not change. "She's into *that* stuff!"

Royal walked out of the kitchen. I heard the front door close. I watched him walk down the path and get in his truck, and drive off.

Mel and Jack converged on me, their voices clattering in my ears.

I ran what I would tell Mike through my mind as I walked along the corridor. He would not like it, but I didn't care.

Voices fell silent as I passed through the Squad Room. A phone rang unanswered. Nobody said a word to me as I maneuvered between desks, heading for Mike's office. I didn't see Royal.

Mike looked up as I came in and half rose to his feet, then sat down heavily. Then he got up and shut his door. I faced him, feeling awkward. Voices rose as a hum in the background. Someone answered the insistently ringing phone.

He took his seat. "Sit, Tiff."

I did. As I put my hands in my lap, I checked the cuffs of my blue and white plaid shirt to make sure they covered the fresh bandages on my wrists. "I know you must have worried," I began.

He came half out his chair again, fists balled. "Worried! I have two units on you and assigned Brad Spacer twenty-four-seven! And you waltz in here as if. . . ." He sat back down hard, reached for his phone and punched a button. A second later he said, "Brad, call off the APB."

I heard Spacer's voice, "Already done."

Mike all but slammed the phone down. I inwardly cringed.

He sucked in a deep breath through his nose and the red of his face returned to near normal. "Talk."

"I thought I had a lead on Lawrence. Didn't pan out."

The way he looked at me, I should have shriveled up like a dead leaf. "You knew how we'd react when you called and your phone went dead, what I would put in motion."

"I figured. But . . . I was tired."

His color rose again. "That's it? You were *tired*? So you snuggled down in bed. . . ." Words obviously failed him.

He was furious, but I wasn't exactly pleased with him, either. "I thought I had a lead, I thought about calling you, then I thought to hell with you."

He took it better than I expected. In fact he calmed down. "What happened with Roy in Granby?"

"What didn't happen with him afterward."

He massaged his chin as he stared at me. I fiddled with a loose thread on the hem on my shirt.

He finally said, "What am I going to do about you, Tiff?"

I looked up and met his eyes. "Nothing. I quit."

I had no choice. Law Enforcement agencies all over the world would continue to look for those little boys, and Mike would waste manpower and resources trying to find Lawrence, but I couldn't do anything about that. I couldn't tell Mike or the FBI Lawrence was alive and living in another dimension, the children were murdered by demons; that, hopefully, it was all over.

Mike and I were through. I expected too much from him. I thought he totally trusted me, but when it came to accusing one of his men, he didn't even consider I could be right. He went through the motions in a desultory manner, but had no intention of investigating Royal. I don't blame him; it was a tough call, and if he had investigated Royal he would have found nothing. But when I fingered Royal, Mike lost faith in me. When he didn't believe me, I lost faith in him. We couldn't discuss it, because after all, I was wrong about Royal, and how could I explain a dead child was mistaken? Yes, the dead see the face of their killer, and Charlie saw a demon who changed his appearance to look exactly like Royal.

I thought Mike and I had a bond formed by a good working relationship, yet when I accused a police officer he forgot the times I was right, when I brought killers to justice. Mike dismissed what I told him about Charlie and Royal, and that dented my ego.

Mike eyed me in a considering kind of way. Then he leaned back, clasped his hands over his belly and nodded.

And that was it. I rose and walked out of his office without another word. I kept my head high as I went through the Squad Room. I didn't look at anyone and kept my expression neutral. But a small sorrow in my chest rode with me as I left the building. I never felt the guys really accepted me, never felt one of the team, but we had a measure of camaraderie I'd not known since I worked for Bermans.

And what the heck would I do for money now?

I had a lot on my mind as I drove home. I needed a job, anything I could get. My work for Clarion PD paid well but infrequently, so I already lived on a shoestring budget. *Had* paid well. I would go back downtown and register with the Temp agencies later in the afternoon. In the meantime, I better scour the Help Wanted ads in the newspaper and online.

One minute a demon-ridden, Lord-saving super-heroine, the next unemployed. Life sucks sometimes.

I parked in the street, went indoors and to the kitchen. There are times when I wish I could redo the living room so I have someplace else to sit and relax. I wonder I haven't worn grooves in the kitchen floor, as often as I'm in there.

I noticed the light on the answering machine blinking furiously and decided I should check messages, although they must be from Clarion PD and I had an idea what they said.

I hunched over the counter and hit the Play button.

"Tiff?" It's Colin."

For a second it was like, Colin, who's he?

"I feel bad about leaving a message, but you don't answer your phone. Look, Tiff, it's not working out. I want a girlfriend I can be with more than once every couple of weeks. And you've been distant. I think you know there's no future for us. I hope we can still be friends."

The old standby: *I hope we can still be friends.* As if that ever works out.

"Um. I gotta go, Tiff. Maybe I'll see you around."

I deleted the message, then listened to three hang-ups and four messages from Clarion PD. I didn't feel bad about Colin dumping me. I *did* feel bad I let a man I really liked, and with whom I had been intimate, be utterly erased from my mind.

Jack breezed into the kitchen. "How are the wrists?" he asked snarkily.

I turned my spine to the counter. "I told you what happened."

"As if we believe you," he said close to my ear.

I jumped. "I've asked you before not to do that, Jack."

He drifted to the kitchen table. "Sorry. I didn't think."

"Nope. It's not a habit of yours. Where's Mel?"

"Upstairs, dreaming of bacon and sausage no doubt."

I bet it wasn't all she dreamed about. After lusting after Gorge, Mel had now seen a spectacular demon at close quarters, in the flesh, not a picture in a newspaper. She would run the experience through her mind for a good long time and pester the life out of me talking about it.

I measured a cup of water into my electric kettle and turned it on. "I quit my job with the PD."

"What?" Jack appeared too close to my shoulder again. I squinted at him through one eye. He backed off. "What are you going to do?"

"Get another job," I said as I opened the cabinet and grabbed the packet of teabags.

He slapped his palms either side of his face. "You'll have to sell the house!"

I got a clean mug and dropped a bag in it. "Don't be ridiculous. The house is paid for. So long as I earn enough to cover utilities and basics, we'll be just fine. I'll worry about property taxes when I get the notice. Though I might have to find a job nearby so I can walk to work."

"Property taxes? But they're due this month, and they're *huge!* How much money *do* you have?"

"Five hundred in Savings. A few dollars in Checking."

Jack relaxed. "Phew. Nothing to worry about, then."

"Wasn't me worrying!" I poured hot water in the mug and dunked my teabag. I paused with the teabag dangling from its string. Money had more value when Jack was alive. "You do realize five hundred dollars doesn't go far these day?"

But Jack was looking through the backdoor. "Something's outside."

Chapter Twenty

I joined Jack and looked through the window. I didn't see anything unusual. "What do you mean, something?"

"For just a second, between the apple trees. It's gone now."

I peered out with my nose inches from the glass. "Yeah, but what did it look like? An animal?"

"A shape, man-sized, kind of blurry."

I held my breath as I gazed intently. Then I saw movement, a small dark shape jutted out from the apple's trunk and disappeared again. It could be a squirrel on the trunk. Or an elbow. I cracked the door and listened. The yard was perfectly silent. Not a bird cheeping, not a chirrup from the grasshoppers. A ray of sun broke free from a sullen sky and I saw a flash, sunlight reflected off metal. My heart lurched.

I went to the kitchen drawer where I kept my Ruger and took off the safety. I returned to the backdoor with the gun in my hand.

Jack eyed the Ruger. "What is it?"

"A demon, I think."

"Him?"

I shook my head.

"How do you know?"

"Why would Royal hide in the backyard?"

"Don't you go out there, Tiff. If anything happened to you, it would kill me."

"Nothing can kill you, Jack," I said softly. I wanted to hug him. The small, rare indication of tenderness evoked the same feeling in my breast.

Why did a demon hide in my backyard? I thought Kien's death put an end to it. They had no right to be here. It was over. The High Lord had returned to Bel-Athaer. Maybe I should not automatically think my visitor was up to no good, but I wasn't going out without my gun.

I swung the door open and stepped outside, leaving it ajar lest I needed to get back in fast. Rain drizzled down now, though the sun still shone in the west and made the raindrops glitter like diamond chips.

Standing on my small concrete patio, in my own backyard, trying to see every which way at once was freakingly scary. It was all so familiar. The scrub oak, small pine, wild mulberry and canyon maple at the back of the lot; the fruit trees to the fore on a piece of mown grass. The leaves of the grapevine had shriveled and scrunched on the brick wall. The yard looked the same as always, but felt like another world.

My heel cracked an acorn and I froze; it sounded too loud. But whoever lurked in the yard knew I was here, so I stepped on the grass and slowly, cautiously walked to my right. Nothing but me moved in my backyard. I stood in the rain a foot from the redbrick wall. Raindrops spattered off the withered vine. The hems of my jeans grew damp from the long, wet grass.

My peripheral vision caught movement. I swung in a crouch. He appeared between the cherry and an apple tree, long red-on-black hair in damp ribbons on the shoulders of his ankle-length black leather coat. Caesar's partner Phaid, who pinned me to the ground and made me, for a few minutes, want him so bad it hurt.

With one arm behind his back, the other curved at his waist, he stopped in front of the trees, and spoke, and although from a distance away and he didn't raise his voice, I heard him. "For the murder of Kein Morté Tescién, I pronounce judgment."

No demon charm in his silken voice, no allure in his glossy eyes; they were cold, hard green emeralds. I lifted my gun and waited as my heart thudded.

He took two paces. I held my gun two-handed, straight-armed, and aimed at his chest. "I didn't murder anybody."

My hair and clothes were sodden. Water trickled down my forehead, hung on my eyelashes. I didn't dare blink my eyes.

"Shall I speak the verdict?" he asked.

When I said nothing, he cocked his head to one side. "What? You have no tongue? Yet, surely you can guess."

And he brought a bloody great sword from behind his back.

Not that it had blood on it, but the thing was huge, a good four foot long from hilt to tip and curved in a crescent. His gaze fondly ran down the gleaming metal, then he flicked it sharply, making raindrops fly. A ball of ice formed in the pit of my stomach.

"Guilty!" he spat.

He came at me with long, loping strides. I kept my aim on him longer than I should, knowing I must fire, now, before he reached me.

He wasn't there anymore.

A hornet stung my upper right arm. Disoriented, I looked and saw a dime-size slit in my plaid shirt, a slit with edges going red.

He moved faster than Royal did in the bowels of Morté Tescién, faster than my eye could see, and he had cut me.

I shuffled my feet, trying to find a defensive stance, but how can you defend yourself against an adversary you cannot see?

"Here I am!" he sang. I spun a fast circle, and he seemed to appear on the patio out of nowhere.

I watched him intently, yet I didn't see him take off. But this time I heard him, a soft *whoosh* of air like the beat of a huge wing.

Ouch! The other arm. Now I had a matching set.

I turned, and caught my foot on my other ankle. Trying to keep my balance, I staggered to one side. Before I could think, he came at me again. I saw his face blink in and out, and felt the sting on my right shin. I clutched my gun, my teeth chattering. Phaid meant to slice and dice and leave me in tiny bloody pieces in my backyard.

Pull yourself together, Tiff. You got out of Bel-Athaer in one piece. You can do this.

Royal came for me.

But he's not here now. You're on your own. You're so big on being the independent woman—you can deal with it.

But the absence of familiar sounds . . . I felt like the rain and I were trapped in a vacuum. My senses strained to hear traffic, music from an open window, a neighbor's voice. I heard only the light patter of raindrops.

He came from the right again. Another tiny nick just above the first. I thought I saw a barely-there break in the rain, as if something pushed the sparkling raindrops aside.

I tried to slow my breathing and find a calm place, but my heart thudded out of control. I tried to forget the lack of background noise and concentrate on the raindrops, listening for any change in the pattern they made as they spattered grass and foliage. Every nerve on my body strained to feel displaced air. And because I listened so intently, I heard Jack's whispering cry: "On your left. Incoming!"

I heard the soft beat of a wing.

I pivoted on the balls of my feet and saw the raindrops slash to one side.

I felt the air move. I tracked a sensation with my gun as it came at me.

I saw what wasn't there, and fired.

He somersaulted through the air, black-red hair streaming, long black coat flapping, like a giant raven tumbling clumsily to the grass, the sword falling from limp fingers. He hit, and rolled, and came to rest on his back with arms and legs sprawled north, south, east and west.

My Ruger dragged my hand down. I made my feet move until I stood over him. His eyes had lost their glitter, but still glowed a bright emerald green, turned to a sky they no longer saw. I kicked the sword away, kicked it again, till it lay a good distance from Phaid's hand. I don't want to describe the head wound. Demon's bleed red, just like men.

"Gotcha," I said, unsurprised my voice sounded hoarse.

I backed to the patio and sat on the edge. I knew I should think about what to do next. The cops would be here soon. But I couldn't move. I sat holding my gun in a grip so tight it hurt. I laid my wrists on my spread knees, letting the gun hang, and dropped my head.

With no warning, the scent of amber and sandalwood surrounded me, and Royal's arms crushed the breath from my lungs.

Royal stood, bringing me upright. "One of your neighbors is talking to Dispatch and others are about to make the same call." He let me go and went to Phaid, watching me, probably to make sure I could stay on my feet. "Go inside. Clean your gun. Do it as fast as you can."

As I stepped on the patio, he crouched, put Phaid's wrists together and with one hand hauled the limp body upright; bent again, and pulled it over his shoulders fireman's style. He bent, took the sword in his free hand.

He was gone in a blur. I went in the house, trying to shake the numbness in my body before it got to my brain.

Jack and Mel were hysterical. They careened around the kitchen, babbling. Then Jack tried to hug me and managed to hug himself inside my body.

"Eew!" I said. "Get out of me, Jack!"

He backed off, batting the air with both hands. "You stupid, stupid woman. What did you think you were doing, going out there?"

"I have the feeling he would have come inside otherwise."

"Oh my, oh my," Mel twittered. "I feel quite faint. I want to throw up."

I burst out laughing. I was still laughing when Royal came back in the kitchen.

"Tiff?"

I couldn't stop. He held me close, but gently. I laughed on his damp jacket till my voice broke on a sob of relief. Jack and Mel were absolutely silent as they gawked at us. I slowly let all the breath in my lungs seep out as

Royal's warmth comforted me, as one arm hugged me tighter and the other hand caressed the nape of my neck beneath my braid.

I took in a breath and pulled back. "Why did he come after me?"

"He came for me, but he wanted to wound me first."

"By killing me?"

He did not reply; his expression and cloudy eyes said it all.

He stroked wisps of hair back from my forehead. "He had to die, Tiff."

"I know. Should I feel bad about it?" I hoped he didn't think I should feel remorse, because I did not. Phaid tried to kill me. He didn't succeed. I won. That made me feel pretty good.

Royal's hands went to my shoulders, squeezed. "No, you should not," he said sincerely.

I still had worries. "I thought it was over when we left Morté Tescién. Are we still in danger? Is anyone else gonna come after us?"

"I think Phaid acted alone."

I studied his expression."But. . . ?"

"My victory guaranteed our escape from Bel-Athaer, nothing more," he said reluctantly.

I pictured Caesar's sneering face. "Others may come after us?"

"They face the might of the High House."

I took his face in my hands and stared into his copper eyes "You didn't answer me."

He rubbed his forehead on mine. "I don't know, Tiff."

He pulled back. "My friends are leaving your neighbor's house," he warned.

He took my Ruger from me and went to the kitchen drawer where I keep it with my cleaning kit. He must have used a little demon speed, because he holstered his Glock and closed the drawer on my Ruger in minutes.

Cleaning the guns was a precaution. If the cops wanted to look through the house, or worse, inspect the weapons they knew we owned, my Ruger and Royal's Glock looked like they had not been fired lately. A forensics test would probably say otherwise, but Royal did not think it would come to that. They knew him, and had no reason to doubt the word of a fellow officer.

"What did you do with. . . ?" I couldn't say his name aloud.

"I stowed him where no one will find him. I'll call the High House; they will send a team for him within the hour."

"You can call Bel-Athaer?"

"I told you, Tiff, we are a modern society. Our technology is a match for yours."

I would say their technology surpasses ours. I'm pretty sure we can't make a phone call to another dimension.

He went to the west windows. "They have no reason to look in your yard, but I moved your lawnmower to cover the blood just in case."

A knock sounded. I wiped at my eyes with the back of my hand. Royal went to the front door.

"We've been here all afternoon, Tom," he said.

I couldn't hear what Officer Tom Murphy said, just the rumble of his voice: "Rumble, rumble, rumble?"

"No. We did hear a car backfire," Royal replied.

"Rumble, rumble."

"I'm not surprised. It made one hell of a bang and you know how the proximity of the mountains can distort and amplify sound."

"Rumble, rumble, rumble, rumble!"

Royal laughed. "That's how it goes. Remember those reports of an explosion last month? A jet, breaking the speed barrier."

"Rumble, rumble? Rumble, rumble."

"No problem. I'll see you tomorrow."

"What a relief," Mel said.

Royal zipped back in the kitchen. "Done." He put his hands on my shoulders and held me away. "Now let's deal with you."

"*Deal* with me?"

"You're soaking. You need dry clothes, and let me look at those cuts."

I looked from one arm to the other, then bent my knee so I could see the back of my shin. "I think he meant to nick me to death."

"Exactly what he intended. The death of five hundred cuts."

"I suppose that's another of your freaking traditions."

"A ritual death reserved for traitors." He took my hand. "Come on."

I meekly let him lead me upstairs to the bathroom. I looked back to see Jack and Mel coming after us. I made a fist at them. Jack pantomimed terror. Mel said, "Oh come on, Jack. Let them have a minute."

I went in the bathroom where Royal told me to strip. I did it. I didn't feel too uncomfortable standing in my bathroom in just my bra and panties. He had already seen me naked, and although I prefer plain, serviceable clothing, I like feminine underwear. These were pale lavender satin overlaid with silver lace.

He dabbed antiseptic on the tiny cuts. It stung so bad I had to clench my teeth. But after he stuck Band-Aids on them, I barely knew they were there. Then he took my chin in a gentle grasp and turned my head to one side, then the other. "Can't do much about the bruising I'm afraid. You are going to look like your boyfriend beat you up."

"What bruising?" I went to the mirror and saw a dark smudge down the side of my face.

"I knocked into you rather hard," he said with an exaggerated wince.

I put my hand to my face. I hadn't noticed how hard he struck me at the time, I was just glad to see him.

Speaking of boyfriends. "Just what did you mean when you burst in to my rescue—*I come to claim what is mine?*" I mimicked dramatically.

He did not answer. I looked at his reflection in the mirror, saw his gaze on my body, and lost any inclination for jocularity. I saw the way in which his eyes changed to a deeper brown with fire in them. The atmosphere in the bathroom became sultry, like a hot, humid August day when you want to doze the afternoon away. He clenched his hands to fists and in two quick strides was against my back, burning down the length of my spine. He pulled me so tightly into his body, an atom couldn't have squeezed between us. "You are mine, my ice maiden," he said thickly.

His lips were butterfly wings on my neck. I think I burned hotter than him, as if fire licked my body, tingling in all the right places. I felt something else, too, pressed into my buttocks through the thick denim of his black jeans.

He picked me up and cuddling me to his chest, took me to my bedroom and lowered me to the bed.

I tried to speak, but his lips got in the way. He breathed in my mouth and I inhaled the sweetness of honey, the spicy heat of cinnamon. His tongue dipped in my mouth, long and narrow like a cat's. I gently bit down on the tip, and he held still till I released it, and caressed it with mine.

No fumbling with clasps and zippers; a gentle tug at my back and hip and I was naked, and I don't know how he got his clothes off without my knowing.

Achingly slow, his heat lapped me as tongue and lips explored my bare skin like velvet fingers, searching, probing. My nipples ached as he teased first one then the other into his mouth. His fingertips found every sensitive place with a delicate, unhurried touch, playing my body until I quivered. I traced hollows and hills of taut satin skin and unyielding muscle and tangled my fingers in his hair; he groaned softly as I gently sucked the hollow of his neck.

As slow, as sweet, he came into me, a hot, smooth heat fiercer than his skin. Supporting himself with one arm, he slipped the other around my hips and lifted them from the bed, and held me to him as we rocked. My muscles joyfully tightened on him, my thighs clasped his hips, my hands his shoulder blades. Until pleasure was a hair away from pain and eclipsed as something divine. My back arched, I cried out.

He stilled. Breathing in the spice of his skin and hair, liquid, knowing I would dissolve and melt away if he let me go, I hung in his arms. And he moved again, just so, and he was right. . . .

. . . .right *there*. Staccato gasps and bubbles of laughter mingled in my throat, until the throb, the pulse, coalesced in my groin and spiraled deliciously through my body, and became too exquisite to be named. My nails dug in his skin as I looked into eyes which blazed copper. He grinned fiercely as his body strained, tensed, went rigid, but only a whispering sigh came from his mouth.

Christ! a distant part of my mind said. *I could die of this.*

Epilogue

———ᵞ———

Royal and I lounged on recliners in my backyard, doing what regular people do during an all too brief Indian summer, catching the last afternoon rays of a fading year. Head back, eyes closed, hair loose and spread in a glittering fan, he nursed a beer. I held open the pages of a book I did not read.

Mel and Jack ogled us from the kitchen door. I had to tell Royal about them soon. I don't know if they watched while Royal and I bounced the bed that first time; it was the last thing on my mind. I didn't ask and they didn't tell. But we did have a long and spirited conversation. Spirited—get it? Actually, I threatened them. If they tried to watch me and Royal when . . . when I didn't want them to, no newspapers, no talk of the outside world, absolutely no socializing. I would totally ignore them. I could do it. For Royal's oh-so delightful company, I could do it.

They sulked for a full day, but caved just the same.

So the Peeping Tom aspect was taken care of, I hoped. But Royal being here so often made life awkward. I couldn't talk to them and had to watch myself lest I react to anything they said or did. And they made the most of that by acting up, and about drove me out of my mind at times.

"How's Lawrence doing?" I asked.

"Taking it in stride." Royal chuckled. "I think his advisors have a handful. He is already asserting his authority. He sent two aides out last week, for Mayberry's double-fudge chocolate ice-cream."

"Mayberry's here in Clarion?"

He nodded lazily.

"Will he bring peace to Bel-Athaer?"

"I do not doubt he will eventually. Gorge smuggled him inside the High House and only his advisors and personal aides know he is there. He's secluded in one wing of the House, where he will go through a good deal of training and tutoring. He'll be presented to the court in a month or two, then word will spread. Everyone in Bel-Athaer will feel him when he comes into his full power."

"When will that be?"

"Five years. Ten. We cannot be sure. If we can keep him safe till then, he will bring the rebel Houses to their knees."

So Lawrence was still in danger. Poor kid.

"Tiff, I've been thinking."

He sounded serious. "You better watch that," I remarked.

He opened eyes which sparked with enthusiasm. "We could open our own agency."

I sat up and swung my legs over the edge of the seat. "Like in private eyes?" Our own agency. *Wow!* I grinned, then lost it. "Isn't moonlighting against precinct policy?"

"I'll resign."

He couldn't mean it. "But you've been a cop forever. How can you up and quit just like that?"

"I would rather work with you."

Hm.

My brow puckered as my suspicious mind thought it through. "I know you're strong on serve and protect—you wouldn't be suggesting we partner up so you can transfer your allegiance to me, would you?"

His face took on a neutral expression.

I bristled. "You are. You think I can't take care of myself."

He sat up, swung his legs and faced me. He took my book from me, laid it on the grass and held my hand. "Is caring for your safety wrong? Call it a demon thing if you like—we cherish our womenfolk."

I looked in his solemn, deep-copper eyes and knew he meant every word. I felt all mushy. *Damn.*

"But that has nothing to do with my suggestion. We'll make a great team, Tiff. Think of the advantages we'd bring to a partnership. With my experience and your talent . . . our own agency is the next logical step. "

"I'll think about it," I said.

As I ate my spicy chicken noodles and tried to read, Mel and Jack decided to go all girlfriend on me. "Are you in love with him?" Mel asked in a dreamy tone.

It was a question I refused to ask myself. Hard as I tried, I couldn't forget the lessons life taught me, what happens when you lower your defenses and unconditionally give yourself to another person. Yet a certain look from his eyes and I all but dissolved. His hands sent delicious sensation clean through me. His heat and scent were as familiar as my own body. I let him slip through barriers no other had breached.

"As if she'd tell us," Jack told Mel. "Asking her is a waste of breath."

"Like we have plenty of that to waste," Mel said, then they went into a fit of giggles.

I looked up from my book. "Can't I just plain enjoy being with a guy?"

"Aw, honey," Mel said, reaching to give me a consoling pat on the shoulder and changing her mind. "You take no notice of us. No reason a girl can't indulge herself with a passionate man who treats her like the center of his universe."

The center of his universe. He did act that way sometimes.

Could he, one day, be the center of mine?

My nosy roommates gave up on the subject. "Are you going to open an agency?" Jack asked.

I wanted to. Royal and I could go anywhere the client required, as long as they paid the expenses. A smart detective with the advantage of strength, speed and sensitive hearing, and a fast learner with an edge all her own— sounded like a win-win situation to me. I doubted we'd be swamped with murder cases, but my ability could still be helpful. The dead are all around us and they're always watching. They can do nothing else.

They whisper to me.

EXTRAS

Meet the Author

Linda D. Welch was born in Hampshire, England, and lived in Idaho, California and New Mexico before settling in Utah. She now lives in a mountain valley, more or less half way up the mountainside, with her husband and two Scottish terrierz. She is not tall and silver-haired and she does not see dead people. What she does see are moose, deer, fox, raccoon, skunk, wild turkey, a huge bird population and a ridiculous amount of snow. When not writing, and depending on the season, she is usually walking the Scotties, filling the bird feeders, futilely attacking the weeds in her garden or shoveling out after a snowstorm. You can visit Linda at http://lindadwelch.com. She looks forward to seeing you there.

If you enjoyed

Along Came A Demon

the next in the series is

The Demon Hunters

A missing Latino lover. Sword-wielding assassins. The nineteenth-century journal of a young girl in what was then Burma. *Very* strange clients. . . .

In The Demon Hunters, Tiff Banks meets two mysterious new clients. She doesn't think they are human beings, and her suspicions are confirmed when the Gelpha High Lord calls them Dark Cousins. What are Dark Cousins? Tiff has no idea. Her partner knows, but won't, or can't, tell her. The Dark Cousin clients are not exactly informative; in fact, they withhold information Tiff thinks could be vital to solving their case. Lives are at risk, and so is her relationship with the one man she's come to trust. Can Tiff's spectral informers help her this time?

You bet.

Turn the page for Chapter One of The Demon Hunters.

Chapter One

—♈—

"Are you sure?"

"Of co . . . not bleeding sure . . . illy cow! All I said w . . . kitty box . . . effin . . . bin . . . food . . . Don't y . . . isten stupid bi. . . ."

The big old green neon sign was on the fritz, and so was charming Freddie Conroy. As it spluttered and spat and frizzed on and off, so did Freddie. I could just make out what he said, although his voice came as a whisper and the Cockney accent didn't help.

I did not linger in Fresno to bring Freddie's killers to justice; I couldn't care less about the disagreeable little man. Anyway, they had already been apprehended, and were doing time in California State Prison. I couldn't do a thing for Freddy—not that I wanted to—but he could do plenty for me.

You would think he'd be glad to finally have someone to talk to after being stuck up there for years, but the Brit was as unpleasant in death as in life.

In May 2000, Freddie's two business partners took him on the roof of the pharmacy and shot him in the back of the head. I doubt they meant to leave him there, but Freddie uncooperatively pitched over the side of the building and got hung up on the big neon sign, which is where Fresno PD found him the next morning.

Unknown to the residents and visitors to Fresno, as they walk the old district, Freddie's still there, up above their heads, likely cussing them out.

My demon lover and I stopped in a downtown café on our way back to Utah, and overheard two elderly women at the next table. Their friend Gertrude Hackenbacher—seriously, it is her name—lost her best friend and companion of eleven years, her cat Pussywillow. Worse, Pussywillow didn't just wander away from home, he was catnapped. My heart immediately went out to the woman. I'd be devastated if my black-brindle Scottish terrier MacKlutzy disappeared, and enraged to the point of committing murder if someone harmed him. Then the ladies mentioned the magic word: reward.

"A cat?" Royal said as he stirred a ton of sugar in his little demitasse coffee cup. I ask you, why get a seriously potent espresso and make it glutinous with sugar?

"I don't care if it's a cat. We've had two assignments since we opened the agency. A thousand bucks is a thousand bucks," I reiterated.

Royal sounded bemused. "We use our powers of deductive reasoning to discover the whereabouts of a cat?"

I swallowed my mouthful of muffin. "I don't mean we spend days here. I just thought, since this Hackenbacher woman lives nearby, we could take a walk about town, starting at her place, ask a few passersby if they saw anything suspicious."

"Sweetheart," Royal said, reaching for my hand, "who would see anything suspicious in someone toting a cat kennel?"

Royal is the first and only person to call me sweetheart, ever. Royal is first with a lot of things. He's the first and only demon I've ever dated, the first to pick me up in his arms like I weigh no more than a couple of pounds, my first partner in my first detective agency. I could go on and on. . . .

Need I mention he's handsome? He's one of those men to whom every woman's eyes are drawn when he walks in the room, and *they* see him as a human male. I see him as he is. His copper and gold streaked hair reaches his shoulder blades when unbound, and when he's excited it swirls and emits sparks, as if full of electricity. His eyes are deep copper-brown, like new pennies, and glint when he moves. He has a demon's angular face and high cheekbones, his skin the palest copper, like a nice tan.

Royal is not human, but neither is he a demon. I just call him that, but not often to his face. I called his people demons long before I knew their true name. They are Gelpha, and they inhabit Bel-Athaer, a world parallel to ours, but only the Gelpha and a few people like me know. Getting my mind round the concept is all but impossible, so I think of Bel-Athaer as a foreign land, one I have never read about. Gelpha have shared our world for centuries, blending with the human population, running businesses, forming relationships, having half-Gelpha, half-human children.

I knew they existed, but a year ago I never thought to take one as partner and lover. Royal is an enforcer for the Gelpha High Lord. He keeps an eye on Gelpha activities here in my world, although he now spends more of his time keeping an eye on me. When I met Royal, I thought he was my enemy, but he turned out to be the best friend I ever had.

I didn't hold out much hope of tracking down the cat, but it was worth a try. Royal had plenty of money, but I insisted on paying my share, and I could no longer help pay for advertising, which so far didn't seem to be doing us any good, anyway.

We could take a few hours to wander Fresno and still get back to Clarion in good time. The catnappers stuffed Pussywillow in the bright-pink, kitten-sized carrier they found on Gertrude's porch. Pussywillow fit it long ago, but grew into a massive, overweight, orange ball of long hair.

I rubbed my thumb over the knuckles of Royal's hand, grinning at him. "Well, no, a cat in a carrier wouldn't stand out, but maybe a pink kitty carrier with the orange fur of a fat enraged cat poking out might grab the attention."

And that's how we came to be watching an apartment above a small florist in downtown Fresno, and how I came to be talking to nasty little Freddie Conroy.

Freddie was the third dead person I spoke to in a roughly three-square-mile area. He might be the one to prove my theory behind opening my detective agency: although not all our cases would involve a violent death, my ability to talk to the dead could still be valuable. The dead see a lot, they've nothing else to do but observe the world going on around them.

But it's not a good idea to put words in their mouths, or ideas in their heads. There can't be many people like me, who see and talk to the violently slain, and the odds of a dead person getting to talk to one of the living are poor. They tend to say what they think I want to hear, just to keep me around. I had to ask the three in Fresno a particular question, and the first two obliged by sending me off on a wild-goose chase. But Freddie was mean and irritable and didn't want me here, so maybe he would tell the truth to get rid of me. Kind of like reverse psychology.

"Shall we?" I asked Royal.

He led the way across the street to the shop, the hot California sun beating down on our heads. July, and Fresno already baked. Next month, the trees lining the streets of the old part of town would start to look sad, and store owners would have to water their curbside planters daily. The florist shop had wide, deep awnings along the front to protect the floral displays clustered about the door.

The door in the alley could be a side entrance to the shop, but I bet it opened to stairs leading to an apartment. Freddie said he saw the occupants take a bright-pink cat kennel from their car and through the door. The orange cat inside was huge, obviously much too big for the little carrier. He also said in the past three days they'd bought cans of cat food, dry kibble and milk from the market a block over.

More than one fat orange cat in a bright-pink kennel would be one hell of a coincidence, but we would be cautious. Freddie could be lying to me.

Royal gave the door an authoritative knock. We waited.

Demons have supernatural hearing. "Someone's in there." Royal grinned at me. "And so is a cat."

I beamed back. "I hope it's Pussywillow."

"Not to mention we'll feel like idiots if it's not."

We could see up a staircase through the narrow window in the door. Nobody appeared, but a male voice spoke through the intercom: "Yes?"

"Termite inspection," Royal said. "We have a report of termite infestation in your block. We need to check your building."

A brief pause, then the man replied: "Did you speak to our landlord?"

"I'm on the phone to him now," Royal lied.

"Then you can tell him we don't have termites."

Royal cocked an eyebrow at me. "You sound positive."

"Yes, I do. I'm a carpenter. I'd know if we had termites. Thank you for calling. Bye."

And the intercom clicked off.

Royal frowned. I heaved a sigh. We leaned against the wall either side of the door. How were we going to get inside the apartment now?

Why didn't we call the police? First, I doubt catnapping placed high on their case list, so response would be slow. Second, as Royal said, we would feel like idiots if the cat in the apartment wasn't Pussywillow—which would not be the first freak coincidence I've run in to—and look like idiots to the local PD. That is bad for publicity. Third, the reward was for the return of Pussywillow, not for providing information leading to his return. Maybe Gertrude Hackenbacher would use the technicality to weasel out of paying us.

Royal smiled. "I have a plan."

"I don't like this. He could take off and get in traffic."

"I won't let him get away."

"Maybe the guy hates dogs. What if he hurts Mac?"

"I won't let that happen either, Tiff."

I squinched up one side of my face. "I don't like it, Royal."

"So you said. Do you have a better idea?"

We were in the deeply recessed entry to the florist shop: me, Royal and Mac. Royal unthinkingly reached out to touch Mac's head. Mac's lips curled off his teeth. Royal took his hand back. "Nice dog. Nice Mac." To me, he said, "I'm going to make him like me if it kills me."

"Well good luck with that. As far as I know, I'm the only person Mac tolerates. I don't think he actually *likes* anyone."

MacKlutzy is the aforementioned Scottish terrier. He's a bumbling, crotchety little animal, and has a streak of determination unrivaled in the doggy world. The first time I left him alone in the house, when he was a puppy, he chewed a huge chunk off the bottom of the bathroom door, trying to escape. Had I not come home when I did, he would have done it too. Royal thought Mac's determination could work in our favor.

Now or never! I carried Mac to the side door, set him on the ground and squatted next to him. I pointed at the door. "Mac! Cat!"

Mac thinks cats would be tasty treats if he ever got hold of one, but he didn't see any cat. He laid his ears back on his skull and glared at me.

"Honest! There's a cat in there, Mac!"

He sniffed at the doorstep and his ears perked a little. He must have found the scent.

I kept urging him, trying to get him excited. "Cat, Mac! *Big* cat!"

After a couple of minutes, he was whining at the door.

"Yes! Cat, Mac! Get the cat!"

Little yips interspersed the whining and snuffling, and he started scratching. Not one of those painted metal types, but good old-fashioned wood, the door didn't stand a chance. Tiny slivers of paint and wood peeled off under Mac's attack. The more I encouraged him, the louder and more frantic he got until he made quite a racket. I hoped the guy upstairs wouldn't turn on his intercom and hear my voice, but there's a specific sound to an intercom, a dead-air sound, even when no person speaks, and I didn't hear it.

The door at the top of the stairs opened and a pair of feet in gray slippers appeared on the top step. I backed away across the alley, into the doorway of a corner boutique in the next block.

I didn't like the next stage. Mac was on his own. Sure, Royal could do the speed-demon thing, whip in and take Mac away, but I don't like to take chances where my dog is concerned.

Peering around the corner, I watched as the door opened and a man came out. Five-eight maybe, long red hair and a goatee, he wore a pair of blue and white checkered pajamas. Mac tried to get past him, but he blocked the dog with his foot. "What the fucking. . . ?"

Mac tried again to get past. The guy edged outside, pulling the door ajar behind him. "Get out of here, you little rat!"

Mac took no notice of the guy, he might not have existed. He focused on the cat he believed to be his legitimate prey. He lunged at the door.

The redhead stepped back, bumping the door open a little more. He yelled at my dog. "Get the fuck out of here, you stupid mutt!"

If there's one thing Mac hates worse than cats, it's being threatened. He recognized the guy's tone. Terriers are fearless. They literally do not perceive any distinction in size or bulk. Something stood between him and a cat and that something threatened him. Mac didn't hesitate, he attacked.

"Oh my God, I am so sorry!" I exclaimed, trying to sound sincere as I rushed across the alley. "I only took my eyes off him for a second!"

The guy clung to the doorframe with both hands and Mac attached to his ankle, wobbling as he tried to keep his balance, swearing up a storm. He tried to shake Mac off. That must have hurt.

"Get it off me!"

"Calm down and hold still. I can't do anything with you shaking him."

I squatted next to Mac. "Mac, bad boy. Let him go."

Mac didn't know what I talked about. Tell him "drop it!" and he'll eventually open his mouth, but he didn't hear it from me. He snarled, a deep throaty snarl muffled by the guy's thick socks.

"Get him off me you stupid bitch or you'll both be sorry!"

I anticipated anger and I've been called a lot worse, so my affront was pure pretense. I straightened to my full height and put ice in my voice as well as my eyes. "Are you threatening me?"

He calmed a little and stood still. "No. But if I have to hurt him to get him off, I will," he said through gritted teeth. "I have a right to defend myself."

Something went between me and the redhead. If you saw a demon move at full speed, it would be just a blur, and you'd tell yourself you imagined it. The door banged open and the guy staggered. I swayed a little.

I squatted beside Mac again. "You're right, and I apologize. If you stand still I'll get him off."

I talked to Mac, who still took absolutely no notice of me.

Another waft of air. I glanced over my shoulder. Royal stood across the street holding a Day-Glo-pink cat carrier.

"Mac, drop it!"

MacKlutzy slowly opened his mouth. I scooped him up in my arms.

The guy backed through the doorway. He hoisted his leg by the ankle and peeled back the sock. "I could sue you."

I picked tiny bits of sock fluff from out of Mac's teeth. "Oh, sorry, did he ruin your sock?" I didn't try to sound apologetic. I didn't care how angry he was. Royal had the cat.

He glared at me. "Keep your fucking dog on a leash, lady!" Then he backed in and slammed the door.

I walked across the street with Mac in my arms. I didn't hurry. Any second now the redhead would discover his prize missing, but what could he do, report a stolen, stolen cat to the cops? Come after us? *Yeah, bring it on, baby.*

I stopped beneath the sputtering neon sign.

"Thanks, Freddie."

"Up yours y . . . fuck. . . ."

I looked up and presented my finger before I walked away. To think, I was going to talk to the pharmacy about getting that sign fixed . . .

Printed in Great Britain
by Amazon.co.uk, Ltd.,
Marston Gate.